D0971326

ALSO BY CHRISTOPHER EDGE

The Many Worlds of Albie Bright

The Jamie Drake Equation

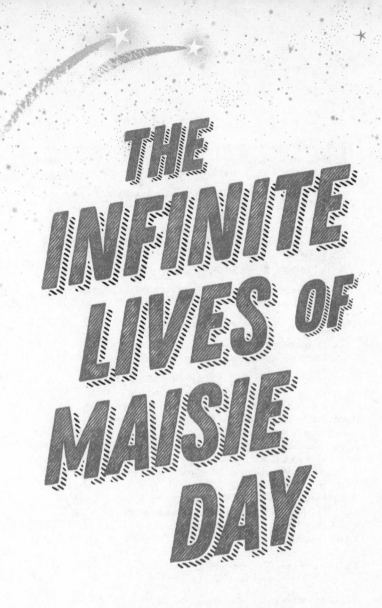

THE INFINITE LIVES OF MAISIE DAY

CHRISTOPHER EDGE

Delacorte Press

Text copyright © 2018, 2019 by Christopher Edge
Jacket art copyright © 2019 by Jamey Christoph

All rights reserved. Published in the United States by Delacorte Press, an imprint
of Random House Children's Books, a division of Penguin Random House LLC,
New York. Originally published in the United Kingdom in paperback and
in slightly different form by Nosy Crow, London, in 2018.

Delacorte Press is a registered trademark and the colophon
is a trademark of Penguin Random House LLC.

Visit us on the Web! rhcbooks.com

Educators and librarians, for a variety of teaching tools,
visit us at RHTeachersLibrarians.com

Library of Congress Cataloging-in-Publication Data
Names: Edge, Christopher, author.
Title: The infinite lives of Maisie Day / Christopher Edge.
Description: New York : Delacorte Press, [2019] | "Originally published in the
United Kingdom in slightly different form and in paperback by Nosy Crow, London,
in 2018." | Summary: On her tenth birthday, super-smart Maisie wakes to a shifted
reality and must work within the laws of the universe and trust the love of her family
to set the world right. Alternate chapters present divergent timelines.
Identifiers: LCCN 2018030846 (print) | LCCN 2018037286 (ebook) |
ISBN 978-0-525-64642-6 (ebk) | ISBN 978-0-525-64640-2 (hardback)
Subjects: | CYAC: Science fiction. | Genius—Fiction. | Self-reliance—Fiction. |
Sisters—Fiction. | Family life—Fiction. | Birthdays—Fiction. | BISAC: JUVENILE
FICTION / Family / Siblings. | JUVENILE FICTION / Science & Technology. |
JUVENILE FICTION / Family / Parents.
Classification: LCC PZ7.E2265 (ebook) | LCC PZ7.E2265 Inf 2019 (print) |
DDC [Fic]—dc23

The text of this book is set in 12.25-point Goudy Old Style BT Roman.

Printed in the United States of America
10 9 8 7 6 5 4 3 2 1
First American Edition

For Chrissie, Alex, and Josie
Forever

To see a World in a Grain of Sand.
And a Heaven in a Wild Flower
Hold Infinity in the palm of your hand
And Eternity in an hour

—*William Blake*

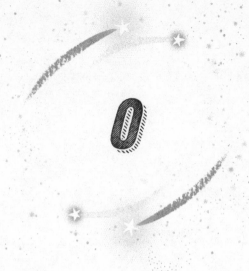

S ome people say that everything began with a Big Bang, but for me, that's the last thing I really remember.

A bang so loud it made me forget everything else.

Everything except for a red balloon floating up into a clear blue sky.

And then darkness.

The insistent beeping of my alarm clock pulls me out of a super weird dream. Something about talking dolphins and the end of the world, I think.

It's funny how that moment in a dream just before you wake up can seem like the most real moment there's ever been. You completely believe that it's true—that it's really happening to you—even if you are talking to a dolphin at the time. But then when you open your eyes, the dream starts to fade right away, and all that you're left with is a strange jumble of thoughts that don't seem to make any sense at all.

Fumbling for the button on top of my alarm clock,

I shake the last of the dream fragments from my mind, my eyes blinking in time with the numbers displayed on the digital screen.

9:00 a.m.

For a second I panic, wondering why nobody has tried to wake me up yet, but then I see the date.

SATURDAY, JUNE 9

It's my birthday.

Jumping down from my cabin bed, I pull open the curtains, and sunlight floods into my room. Through the window I can see the gazebo that Mom and Dad have bought for my birthday party laid out across the lawn beneath protective plastic sheets, just waiting now for Dad to put it up. Over the back fence I can see the railway tracks, and beyond that the backs of the shops that lead up Cheswick Hill, the whole scene bathed in perfect summer sunshine.

I can't stop myself from grinning. Today is going to be the best day ever. I'm ten years old.

The ancient Greek philosopher Pythagoras thought the number ten was the most important number in the world. He basically invented math using it and believed

4

that the whole universe was built out of numbers. Pythagoras said that the number ten contained the key to understanding everything. If this is true, being ten years old is going to be pretty cool.

Maybe now that I'm ten, Mom and Dad will let me go to the shops on my own or even stay up late, just like Lily.

Lily's my older sister. She's fifteen and she hates me.

Mom and Dad say that Lily doesn't hate me. They say she's just a bit stressed at the moment because she's studying for her A-levels for university, but I don't think that's a very good excuse. I passed those exams when I was seven, getting a distinction in physics, chemistry, and math. Now I'm studying for a bachelor of science in mathematics and physics.

The thing is, I'm "academically gifted." Apparently this puts me in the top 2 percent of the population. That doesn't mean I'm smarter than everybody else. I'm absolutely terrible at French. I just love learning about how the universe works. Lily thinks this makes me a freak.

Like I said, she hates me.

Pulling on my robe over my pajamas, I head down the stairs. The house is so quiet. Usually Dad's already in the kitchen by now, noisily cooking up his Saturday-morning pancake breakfast while Mom sits at the kitchen table reading the newspaper.

I turn right at the bottom of the stairs, heading down

5

the hallway and into the kitchen. Beneath my bare feet, the black-and-white tiles covering the floor feel freezing cold. I shiver. The kitchen table is deserted, the frying pan standing silent as the empty counters gleam. There's nobody here.

I peer through the patio doors that lead out into the backyard, wondering for a second if Mom and Dad have sneaked out there to start putting up the gazebo for my party later today, but there's nobody there either.

Maybe they are hiding somewhere and are going to jump out any minute singing "Happy Birthday."

"Mom! Dad!" I call out. "Where are you?"

I stand still for a moment, ready to look all surprised when they suddenly appear. But nobody jumps out. The grin I've been wearing since I opened my bedroom curtains is slowly starting to fade. If Mom and Dad think this is funny, I've got news for them.

The living room is just as empty as the kitchen, the TV turned off and not a cushion out of place on the sofa. I'm not surprised that Lily's not up yet, as she doesn't usually surface until after ten on the weekend. This is because she's a teenager and the hormones in her brain make her sleep late. Maybe that will start happening to me now that I'm ten. Now that I'm ten, everything might change.

I've done a loop of the downstairs now: hall, kitchen, living room, and back to the hall. If Mom and Dad are hiding somewhere ready to give me a birthday surprise, then they're running out of rooms. Our house really isn't that big.

Standing at the bottom of the stairs, I call out again.

"Mom! Dad! This isn't funny. Where are you?"

Still no answer—just a creepy silence that seems to fill the house. I shiver, even though sunlight is streaming through the arch of tinted glass at the top of the front door behind me. Where is everyone? They wouldn't have gone out without me. The excitement I felt when I sprang out of bed has now turned into a nagging sense of worry. I race up the stairs, two steps at a time, wanting this stupid game of hide-and-seek to be over already.

Heading around the landing, I push open the door to Mom and Dad's bedroom.

The room is still in darkness, the curtains drawn against the morning sun, but in the light spilling in from the landing I can see that nobody's here. The bedspread is pulled neatly across Mom and Dad's king-size bed. It doesn't look like it's even been slept in.

The twisting worry that's been coiling inside my stomach is now tightening into a tense knot of fear.

Doubling back along the landing, I glance back inside my bedroom and then peer around the bathroom door too, just to double-check. But both rooms are empty. The only living thing I can see is a spider scurrying toward the faucets when I pull the shower curtain back.

I shiver again, the sunlight streaming through the

bathroom window seeming to lack any kind of warmth. Something's not right.

Back on the landing, I glance toward the second flight of stairs that lead up to Lily's room in the attic. A NO ENTRY sign is stuck to the wall at the bottom of the stairs, and beneath this Lily has written *NO SISTERS ALLOWED.*

She means me.

I wouldn't normally dare to go anywhere near Lily's room on a Saturday morning. Her rage can be positively volcanic if her weekend sleep is disturbed. But this isn't a normal Saturday. It's my birthday, and I want to know where everyone is.

"Lily!" I shout up the stairs, my words echoing off the empty walls. "Are you up yet?"

There's no answer.

"Lily?"

More silence.

I glance at the NO ENTRY sign and then shake my head. This is an emergency.

Taking a step forward, I start to climb the stairs. Inside my head, I quickly flick through the excuses I'll use when Lily freaks out at me for waking her up. I don't know what I'll do if she's not in her room.

Our house is usually filled with noise. This silence is really starting to get to me.

Then the doorbell rings.

I jump in surprise, but as soon as I realize what this means, a sudden wave of relief washes over me. This must be Mom and Dad. They must've got up early to get things ready for my party and then realized that they needed something from the shops. Leaving me and Lily in bed, they popped out and are now back with bagfuls of party stuff and need me to let them in.

I race back down the stairs, skipping around the landing and then barreling down the second flight of stairs. It's time to get my birthday started at last.

As I reach the hallway, the sound of the front doorbell seems to stretch out as if someone has left their finger on it for too long. Then it stops abruptly, and the air hums with absolute silence again.

It must be broken.

Feeling kind of puzzled, I fix a smile to my face, eager to find out exactly what Mom and Dad have got me from the shops.

But when I open the front door, this smile is suddenly eclipsed as my lips stretch wide in a silent scream. The sound of my cheery hello curdles in my throat as I look in horror at the scene outside.

There's nobody there.

But worse than that, there's nothing there.

No Mom. No Dad. No car parked in the driveway. No driveway. No street. No houses.

Nothing at all.

Just an empty black space that goes on forever.

I stare into the darkness, trying to make sense of the impossibility of what I can see.

It doesn't work.

I slam the door shut before my brain explodes.

Gasping for breath, I stand there swaying, my hand still gripping the door handle as I try to work out what's going on.

Looking down, I see a rainbow stripe of colors dappling the polished floorboards, the sunlight streaming in through the tinted glass creating this shifting pattern. But when I opened the front door, there wasn't any sun in the sky. There wasn't any sun. There wasn't any sky. There wasn't anything.

Feeling really frightened now, I back away from the door. If there's nothing out there, who was ringing the doorbell?

Stumbling down the hall, I retreat to the kitchen, slamming the door behind me to try to block out what I've just seen. Still shaking, I slump against the kitchen table, my fingers trembling as I cling to its edge to stop myself from falling down.

What's happening?

"Happy birthday, Maisie!"

With a broad smile on her face, Mom slides a pile of envelopes across the kitchen table toward me. Behind her, Dad glances over his shoulder with a grin, still keeping one eye fixed on the banana pancake that's cooking in the frying pan. The molecules that make it smell sticky sweet weave their way from the stove to the odor receptors in my nose, making my stomach rumble in anticipation.

"Thanks, Mom," I say, looking down at the oversize envelope at the top of the pile. I immediately recognize Mom's handwriting, my name written in large letters across the silver envelope.

Maisie

"Go on," Mom says. "Open it."

As I turn the envelope over, I can see that it's kind of lumpy in one corner and instantly realize what this means. Trying to keep a smile on my face, I rip the envelope open and pull out an enormous birthday card.

On the front, there's a picture of a space rocket zooming through a starry sky, the constellations arranged to spell out the words HAPPY BIRTHDAY. And fixed to the top corner is a bright blue button with a big number ten printed inside a star.

Ignoring the button, I quickly open the card, trying not to blush as I read the message inside.

> To Maisie
> Hope your birthday is out of this world!
> We're so proud of you. Have a fantastic day.
>
> All our love,
> Mom and Dad
> xxx

Mom looks at me hopefully as I set the card on the table.

"I took forever choosing it. So many of these birthday cards for girls nowadays have such silly stuff on them—glittery unicorns and fairies and things. I wanted to choose one that was just right for you. I do hope you like it, Maisie."

I nod, even though the constellations aren't exactly astronomically accurate.

"It's perfect, Mom. Thanks."

"I wasn't sure about the button. Ten's not too old for a button, is it?"

"Stop fussing, Laura," Dad says, leaning across the table to slide the banana pancake onto my plate. I look up at him with a grateful smile. "Maisie doesn't mind what her card looks like—it's the birthday presents that she's waiting for."

As the full force of the banana pancake smell hits my nostrils, I feel an adrenaline rush of excitement at Dad's mention of my birthday presents.

It's true. I don't mind that Mom got me a birthday card with a button, even though they're really just for little kids. If Mom and Dad have got me the present that I've set my heart on, I'll forgive them anything.

I've dropped so many hints, leaving copies of *New Scientist* open on the kitchen table and pinning articles to the fridge. I know they said they couldn't afford to spend a fortune on my birthday present, but I hope Mom and Dad got me the kit I need to help me build my own nuclear reactor.

It all started when I watched this documentary about

this kid who built a nuclear reactor in his garage when he was a teenager, and it kind of inspired me. Now I'm planning to be the first person in the world to crack the power of cold fusion.

When I first told Mom and Dad that I wanted to build a nuclear reactor, they kind of freaked out, worrying about radioactive waste and stuff like that. Dad said he liked the fact I was getting interested in sustainable energy, but he didn't want me blowing up the house.

I told Dad he didn't have to worry. You see, most nuclear reactors work by splitting atoms. This is called nuclear fission and releases a huge amount of energy in the form of heat. Inside a normal nuclear reactor, the temperature can reach over 600 degrees Fahrenheit. That's hot enough to melt lead!

And then there's nuclear fusion, which is even hotter. Take a look up at the sun. All the light you can see, all the heat that you feel is being produced deep inside the sun when smaller hydrogen atoms fuse together to create larger helium atoms. The energy that this releases is what powers the sun and every star in the sky.

When I explained all this to Dad, I could see that he was starting to get *really* worried, so I quickly explained that the kind of nuclear reactor I was planning to build was completely different. Cold fusion does what it says on the tin. Nuclear reactions at room temperature, not even hot enough to melt the butter in Dad's frying pan. No radioactive waste, no chance of explosions. All the energy you need—totally safe and clean.

The only problem is nobody's quite figured out how to make cold fusion work yet. Tons of scientists have tried, but recently I was reading about this experiment that NASA is building, and it gave me a great idea. I drew Mom and Dad a diagram of my plans for a DIY reactor and explained how the cold fusion process using the weak nuclear force would be completely safe.

To be honest, I don't think Mom and Dad understood what I was telling them, but when I said that all I really wanted for my birthday was a backward wave oscillator, a hydrogen generator, and fifty rolls of aluminum foil, they said they'd think about it.

That was four weeks ago, and now it's my birthday.

"Can I open my presents yet?" I ask eagerly.

"Not yet," Dad laughs, retreating to the stove to ladle another dollop of batter into the pan. "Eat your breakfast first. And you've got the rest of your birthday cards to open too."

With a grin, I squirt a trail of golden syrup across my pancake. If Mom and Dad got me what I need, I might be able to harness the power of a star in the old freezer in the garage.

I'm just taking my first mouthful of pancake and

thinking about how I'll be able to hook up the hydrogen generator when the door bangs open, causing Mom to jump halfway out of her chair.

Lily flounces into the kitchen. She's wearing a long-sleeve T-shirt that almost reaches her knees, a picture of some eighties pop star printed on the front.

"Morning, Lily," Dad says, giving the frying pan a shake. "Can I interest you in a pancake?"

Then he does a double take as he notices what she's wearing.

"Is that my Cure T-shirt?"

Lily frowns as she flops down in the chair next to mine.

"I borrowed it," she says, fiddling with the hem of one of the sleeves. She tugs it down over her wrist. "I didn't think you'd mind."

"I don't," Dad replies with a shake of his head. Picking up a spatula, he flips over the pancake that's starting to sizzle in the pan. "But maybe ask next time, okay?"

Lily sighs with a roll of her eyes. Then she turns toward me and pushes an envelope across the table.

"Happy birthday, sis."

"Thanks, Lily," I say, feeling kind of surprised. "I didn't think that you'd remember."

"Well, it was kind of difficult to ignore with everyone talking about it all the time," Lily replies. "I mean, you'd think you were the first person in this family to hit double figures, with the fuss everyone's been making."

"That's not true, Lily," Mom says, reaching out to rest her hand on top of Lily's arm.

"It is," Lily insists, her voice almost pained as she snatches her arm away. I watch the smile on Mom's face crack a little. "I never had any of this for my tenth birthday," she says, gesturing toward the patio doors, through which the poles and plastic sheets for the gazebo can be seen laid out across the lawn. "You just took me and my friends to see some stupid cartoon at the movies."

"That was different," Mom says, keeping her voice calm even as her rejected hand trembles in midair. "You wanted to do something with your friends on your birthday, but Maisie . . ."

Mom's voice trails off. It's okay. She doesn't need to say it because I know the rest of the sentence, anyway. I don't have any friends.

The only people coming to my party today are members of my own family. Mom, Dad, and Lily, Grandma Day and her friend Elsie, Aunt Maggie, Uncle Colin, Auntie Pat, Grace and Jack, all my other aunties and uncles, and the rest of my cousins too, even baby Alfie. All ages from eight months to eighty years old, but there's only going to be one person who's ten, and that's me.

You see, because I don't go to school, I don't have a ready-made gang of friends like Lily. She's always going over to her best friend Sophie's house or inviting Sophie, Daisy, and the rest of her friends over to ours. They stay

17

up in Lily's bedroom for hours on end. They're supposed to be studying for their exams, but seem to spend most of their time OMG-ing at the tops of their voices.

Sometimes I hang around the bottom of the stairs trying to figure out what they're actually doing up there. But I can never quite hear what they're talking about, just the occasional boy's name mixed in with squeals of excitement.

And when Mom sends me upstairs to ask if they want a snack or a drink, Lily always gives me the deadeye—the room going instantly quiet as soon as I walk in.

I used to think Lily's best friend, Sophie, was nice. She always used to talk to me when I went up to Lily's room. Sometimes I even started to think that she could be my friend too.

What used to happen was Sophie would grab hold of her science textbook and flick to the answer section at the back. Then she'd fire questions at me, and everyone would cheer when I got them right—everyone except for Lily. How old is the universe? Which fossil fuel produces the most carbon dioxide? At what speed does electromagnetic radiation travel in a vacuum? It wasn't a big deal. They were only simple questions. But it still felt kind of special to have the chance to hang out with Lily's friends, even if it was just for a little while. I thought Sophie liked me.

But then, one time, I hung outside Lily's door for too

long when Mom sent me upstairs with the snacks and the drinks.

"Oh my God, Lily," I heard Sophie say, the sound of her voice squeezing through the half-closed door. "Your little sister is such a freak. She's practically autistic."

I stood there at the top of the stairs, the glasses of milk and a plate piled with cookies trembling on the tray as I waited for Lily's reply.

I don't know what I wanted her to say. To stick up for me, I suppose. To tell Sophie that I wasn't a freak. There's nothing wrong with being autistic, but I'm just academically gifted. But my sister didn't say a thing.

I left the tray at the top of the stairs. Mom didn't make me go up to Lily's room after that.

So this is why Mom and Dad have invited the whole family to my birthday party. They think it will help me forget that I don't have any friends.

"Never mind whose tenth birthday was the best," Dad says, trying to keep the peace just like he always does. He slides the latest pancake out of the frying pan and onto the plate in front of Lily. "Have a banana pancake."

Lily curls her lip as she inspects Dad's culinary creation. I've only just started mine, but I already want another one. They're just so delicious.

"I don't want a banana pancake," Lily says, pushing the plate away. "I just need some toast and a coffee."

Dad looks kind of hurt. Banana pancakes are his specialty.

"Are you sure?" he asks. "Do you know that bananas are the perfect brain food? It's something to do with all the albino acids they've got inside them."

I think Dad's been reading my *New Scientist* again. He might be a wiz when it comes to technology, but he doesn't know the first thing about biology.

"Amino acids," I say.

"That's right, amino acids," Dad agrees. "It said so in one of Maisie's magazines. Apparently, these amino acids can boost your brain function and even stop you from getting stressed." He gently pushes the plate back toward Lily. "Your exams are just around the corner. Why don't you try a bit of banana pancake? It might help."

Actually, I think *New Scientist* said it was the magnesium in bananas that reduces stress, but before I can tell Dad this, Lily just explodes.

"You're the one making me stressed," she says, spitting out the words as she pushes her chair back with a screech. "Going on about my exams when I've just got out of bed. I only wanted a stupid piece of toast."

"Lily!" Mom says.

But my sister just springs out of her seat.

"Don't you see? It doesn't matter how many banana pancakes I eat for breakfast!" she shouts, crossing the kitchen in a handful of strides. "I'll never be as clever as Maisie."

Storming out of the room, Lily slams the door behind her.

Mom and Dad stare at each other in shock as the sound reverberates around the house.

It might be my birthday, but as usual, Lily's managed to make it all about her.

3

I stare at the pile of envelopes on the kitchen table, my name written across each one.

Today's my birthday. I should be opening these cards with Mom, Dad, and Lily here, but instead I'm all alone. The room seems to hum with an ominous silence. Where is everyone?

What I saw when I opened the front door was like something out of a nightmare.

I look around the kitchen. Beneath the oven hood, the black-and-silver stove top gleams, no sign of any of the usual spills and splatters from Dad's Saturday-morning pancake breakfast. On either side of it the countertops stand empty, the plates and mugs all neatly stacked or hanging in place from the racks on the wall. The fridge-freezer, the microwave, the dishwasher, even the sink. Everything is exactly where it should be. And through the patio doors that lead out into the backyard, the plastic sheets covering the gazebo sparkle with dew under the early-morning sunshine.

But is any of this real?

When you're dreaming, you think that what you see, what you hear, what you can feel is real, even though the dream is all happening in your mind.

Is that what's happening here? Am I still dreaming?

I read that one way you can tell whether you're really awake or still in a dream is to perform a reality check. This can just be a simple action that can help you to confirm if what you're experiencing is real.

Looking down, I slide my finger beneath the flap of the lumpy envelope at the top of the pile, feeling the paper tear as I rip it open, and pull out an outsize birthday card.

On the front of the card there's a picture of a space rocket zooming through a starry sky, silvery lines linking the constellations as they spell out the message HAPPY BIRTHDAY. And fixed to the top corner is a birthday button with a big number ten printed inside a star.

Unfastening the button from the front of the card,

I steel myself, getting ready to perform my own reality check. If this is all a dream, there's one way to find out.

I jab the button's pin into the end of my thumb.

"Ouch!"

Wincing, I watch as a droplet of blood wells from the pinprick. I squeeze the end of my thumb to try to deaden the pain, and the droplet falls onto the front of my birthday card, leaving a brand-new red planet shining among the stars.

This feels pretty real to me.

I shake my head. Maybe I just had some kind of temporary blackout before, a glitch in my brain that meant I couldn't process what I was seeing properly when I opened the front door. But I need to make sure.

Pocketing the button, I push my chair back, feeling the cold tiles beneath my feet as I cross the kitchen to reach the patio doors.

Gazing through the glass, I can see the flower beds blooming red, yellow, and blue, the blossoms on the trees framing the green leaves with a powdering of pink. And in the glass there's a faint reflection of my face, a frightened look in my eyes as I stare out on this perfect scene.

I know that the only reason I can see any of this is because of the sun that's shining down. The green grass, the pink blossom, the sparkle of the plastic sheeting thrown over the gazebo—everything that I can see is a result of photons of light reflecting off these things and traveling to hit my eyes. Even the faint reflection of my face is caused by some of these photons hitting my skin and bouncing back to hit the glass. Without the sun, I wouldn't be able to see any of this.

But a shiver runs down my spine as I remember that infinite blackness I saw when I opened the front door.

Scientists don't accept the result of an experiment until the experiment has been repeated and gives the same result. If you repeat the experiment and get a different result, then you know that something's wrong.

If I want to find out if the sun *is* really shining through the glass, I'm going to have to open the patio door.

My throat feels dry as I reach down to turn the key in the lock. It's ridiculous. All the evidence from my eyes is telling me that all I'll find waiting outside is the backyard, same as it always is. But I can't stop my fingers from trembling as I take hold of the door handle, a faint smear of blood now visible on my thumb.

It's time to find out what's real.

Turning the handle, I push open the door.

Even though my mind is half expecting it, it doesn't stop the sight I see from hitting me like a punch in the face.

There's no sun shining down on our backyard. No green grass, no blooming flowers, no pink blossoms in the

25

trees. No backyard. Just an empty black space that begins at the doorstep and stretches into infinity in every direction that I look.

My fingers tighten around the door handle, every instinct inside screaming at me to slam the door shut. But I resist. I've got to make sense of this.

It's as though our house has been launched into the depths of space. But what I can see outside the back door isn't a starry sky like the one on the front of my birthday card. This is an empty universe, not a single star in the sky.

Swaying slightly, I cling to the handle, feeling as though I could just float out into this infinite blackness.

There's this stuff called Vantablack, which is the darkest material ever invented. Scientists make it out of carbon nanotubes—teeny-tiny tubes of carbon, thousands of times thinner than even a human hair—that are woven together. If you shine a light at something that's made out of Vantablack, the light just gets lost in this forest of nanotubes, so all you see is an empty black space where the object should be. It's not just black—it's super black.

That is what it looks like outside.

Still clinging tightly to the door handle, I reach out with my free hand, pushing it against the darkness. There's no resistance, no change in temperature as my hand moves from inside to out. But as I push against the darkness, I can't help feeling scared that the darkness will push back.

I crouch down, bracing myself against the doorframe as I lean forward. I need to see how far this blackness goes. There might be no world outside, but can I even see where it might have gone? My stomach lurches as I crane my neck in every direction, desperately searching for any sign of life in this infinite blackness.

But that's all I can see. Darkness, everywhere.

Shaking, I haul myself back from the edge, my bare feet slipping against the black-and-white tiles as I retreat from the door.

If you can successfully repeat an experiment, then the evidence supporting it grows.

This is real.

Outside my house there's an empty void, and I don't know if Mom, Dad, and Lily are ever coming home.

As I stare out into the infinite blackness, the shape of the doorframe seems to blur.

I rub my eyes, thinking that maybe the signals from the optic nerves to my brain are getting confused by this super blackness. That's what happens if you stare at Vantablack for too long—with so little light reflected, your brain can't figure out what you're looking at. All surface details disappear. A crumpled-up piece of paper looks completely flat when it's coated in Vantablack.

But then I realize that the doorframe isn't blurred. There are black blobs floating around it. The darkness is coming inside.

Frozen, I stare as these blobs hover on the threshold. I can see only the ones that are silhouetted against the white doorframe, flat disks of absolute blackness that seem to slowly pulsate as they float inside.

Six . . . seven . . . eight . . . nine . . . ten . . .

More of them keep coming—invisible against the darkness of the abyss until the moment they float inside and are framed against the white molding of the patio doors.

The intensity of the blackness hurts my eyes. It's like a nothing-space, a complete absence of any light. I can't even seem to focus on the blob-like shapes as some hover above the shoe rack that's standing next to the patio doors. On this, Dad's big black rain boots look almost muddy brown in contrast.

Then the closest blob touches the top of a boot and I watch, horrified, as an impossible blackness spreads across the surface of the entire rain boot. I can see it transforming in front of my eyes, changing from a real thing I can see into a flat, two-dimensional shape.

Its darkness hurts my eyes. There's no light reflecting back—just an empty black space where Dad's rain boot used to be.

And the black blob grows larger, almost shivering with pleasure as it floats forward again.

Still crouching down, I feel my stomach flip and choke back a mouthful of sick as more of these blobs flood through the open door. I watch the white molding frame slowly eaten away until only darkness remains. And as the blobs touch the black-and-white kitchen tiles, each one is transformed into a square of absolute blackness, the emptiness advancing across the room in a relentless tide. The outside is coming in and erasing everything that it finds.

It's like the nature program I watched on TV that showed how mold spreads. They set up lots of time-lapse cameras in an abandoned house and recorded how a tiny spore of black mold in the bathroom grew into a black tide of fungus that slowly took over the entire house.

I stare in horror as these blobs of absolute blackness spread across the kitchen, the darkness shape-shifting as it devours everything it touches.

This seems like a nightmare, but the bitter taste of sick in my mouth tells me that it's real. I've got to get out of here.

Scrambling backward, I turn toward the kitchen door, and that's when things start to get *really* weird.

Ahead of me, I can see the door that leads to the hall, still closed from when I slammed it shut, but this picture seems stretched as though I'm looking at it through the wrong end of a telescope. Our kitchen isn't that big, but the door seems to be getting smaller with every second that passes as it recedes into the distance.

I shake my head, my brain unable to process the information it's receiving.

One time, when I was little, I got an infection in my inner ear and had to stay in bed for a week. I felt sick and dizzy all the time, and couldn't even stand up without falling down. It was like everything was spinning and moving around, even when I was completely still. Eventually the infection went away, but I'll never forget how strange it made me feel.

That's how I feel right now as I watch the black-and-white squares tiling the kitchen floor seem to stretch to the horizon.

I glance back over my shoulder, a fresh wave of nausea welling in my throat as I see what's behind me.

Everything's gone. It's like the kitchen is being peeled inside out, the walls, floor, and ceiling disappearing until only darkness remains. And it's speeding up.

The voice inside my head is screaming now, telling me that I've got to get out of here.

Turning back toward the door, I try to scramble to my feet but find I can barely even lift my head as the force of gravity pushing me down suddenly intensifies. Twisting my neck, I see the spotlights in the ceiling overhead stretch into arrows of light as the room keeps expanding.

Nothing makes any sense. I try to drag myself forward, the floor tiles beneath my fingers almost scorching to the touch. Sweat slicks my forehead. I can feel it running down my face, stinging as it mingles with my tears. I open my mouth to shout for Mom and Dad, but no sound comes out, just an empty howl of silence.

My birthday button falls from my pocket and I watch as it skitters across the floor. For a second, it's close enough to touch, but as my fingers start to close around it, the button fades into the distance. Everything's accelerating—the room around me turning into a universe.

Scientists think our universe started out as a tiny seed. A bubble of space-time—a trillion-trillion-trillion times smaller than a grain of sand—seething with all the energy and matter that would eventually create everything in the universe. When the Big Bang happened, this tiny bubble suddenly got very big, very fast. In less than a second, it grew from the size of a subatomic particle to a space thousands of millions of miles across. And since then it's just kept on expanding.

But as I watch the kitchen door dwindle into infinity, it seems like the kitchen is exploding even faster than this.

My head's spinning. I don't know why any of this is happening. Today was meant to be the best day ever, but reality has turned into a nightmare.

Some scientists think that reality is everything that

would still be here even if there were nobody around to experience it. I don't know where Mom, Dad, and Lily have gone. The only person left now is me. If I close my eyes, will this nightmare be over?

Snatching a fearful glance behind me, I see an absolute blackness lapping at my heels. I'm dangling on the edge of infinity, and if this darkness touches me, I know that I'll be gone.

With a last desperate lunge, I fling myself forward, closing my eyes as I reach for the handle of a door that's half a universe away.

And then I turn it.

Warm sunlight hits my skin as I step out into the garden, an instant tingle that turns my goose bumps into memories. I'm wearing my favorite T-shirt, the white one with a sequined star on the front, and the new jeans that Mom bought me for the party. It's going to be a perfect day.

Inside the kitchen, Mom's busy icing my birthday cake. I think that's what she's doing, anyway—she wouldn't let me see, just shooed me out of the kitchen when I tried to take a look.

"Go and give your dad this cup of coffee," she said, handing me a steaming cup. "He looks like he could do with one."

Standing at the top of the patio steps, Dad's scratching his head as he studies the piece of paper in his hand. On the lawn, the plastic sheeting has now been peeled back, trapped droplets of dew still sparkling beneath it as the white canvas canopy of the gazebo is laid out in a neatly folded square. Next to it, a jumble of poles and plastic struts has been emptied across the grass. It doesn't look like Dad has made much progress putting it up yet.

Hearing my footsteps, Dad looks up from his sheet of paper and greets me with a rueful smile.

"Cup of coffee—lovely," he says, reaching out to take the mug from my hand. "I think my brain needs a caffeine injection to help me make sense of these incomprehensible instructions."

"Can I take a look?" I ask.

Dad nods, relieved to hand over the responsibility as he takes a slurp of coffee.

"I'm afraid we might have to have your birthday party inside if I can't figure this out, Maisie. I think there's an important piece missing. I told your mom we shouldn't have gone for a budget gazebo."

Shading my eyes from the sun, I take a closer look at the instructions. There are no words anywhere on the page, just a sequence of diagrams laying out the different parts for the gazebo and showing how they fit together. Dad's still stuck on the first diagram, a spiderweb of poles and joints that slot together to make a frame for the roof.

"I can't seem to find that stupid connector," Dad says, leaning forward to tap the center of the diagram. Dad's pointing at the central joint, an octopus-like piece of plastic that the roof poles are supposed to fit into, the plastic rods radiating off it like bicycle spokes from the hub of a wheel.

Glancing up from the instructions, I look again at the jigsaw of pieces laid out on the lawn. In among the maze of poles, joints, and struts, I notice a couple of parts that look different from the picture—two white plastic joints shaped like stubby crosses.

Reaching down to pick up these pieces, I turn them over in my hand, noticing how they match each other exactly. Then, with a satisfying click, I slot the two pieces together, the crosses now transformed into the eight-way connector that Dad has been searching for.

I hold up this stubby white octopus of plastic.

"I think this is it."

Dad grins.

"Thanks, Maisie," he says, setting down his cup of coffee and then taking the piece from me. "I couldn't see the forest for the trees." Grabbing hold of the nearest of the poles, he slides this into the connecting joint, twisting it with a click to secure it into position. "How about you help me with the rest of this? We'll get this gazebo up much faster if we work together."

Even though I'm itching to head back inside to open my presents, I nod, not wanting to miss out on this chance to spend some time with Dad. He hasn't been around much lately because of work, and there's something I really want to ask him.

Dad's a video game designer. If you've ever played *Fun Kart Fury* or *The Legend of Zombie Tower*, then you've played one of my dad's video games. He didn't make them on his own, of course. There's a whole team of animators, programmers, artists, and writers who work with him too. But Dad's the person who's in charge of making the game a reality.

At the moment, he's working flat out to get this new game he's designed finished in time for Christmas. That means he's working most weekends and hasn't been getting home until late at night. Mom calls this the Crunch, but she still made sure that Dad took today off for my birthday.

Lily and I used to have so much fun testing out demos of the latest games that Dad was working on. We'd race around in *Fun Kart Fury* throwing bombs to knock each other off the track and then collapse in a giggling heap when a glitch in the game made our avatars start farting whenever we tried to accelerate. That's what it sounded like, anyway. Dad used to give us a dollar for every bug we found, so that game gave me a big pocket-money bonus.

Lily doesn't play video games with me anymore. She says she's too busy with her exams. I miss the old Lily.

"Dad," I say, holding the next pole steady as he slides it into the central joint of the roof frame. "Why's Lily so angry about my birthday party?"

Twisting the pole to lock it into place, Dad shakes his head.

"She's not angry about your party, Maisie. Lily's a teenager. She's angry about everything. You see, when you hit puberty—"

I cut Dad off before he starts embarrassing the both of us.

"I know all about puberty, Dad," I tell him. "I did it in biology. And Mom has explained all the annoying parts about being a girl."

"Right," Dad says, his Saturday-morning stubble unable to disguise the blush that's now creeping across his cheeks. "Well, you know that when you're a teenager, you've got a lot of changes going on. Not just your body, but your emotions too. Lily's not angry at you or me. She just got up on the wrong side of the bed today."

I wish that were true, but the truth is, Lily's been mad at me for longer than this. I think it all began when I started school.

That's when people first began to realize that I was "academically gifted." Mom had already taught me how to read and write at home, so I thought that when I got to school, I'd be able to get started on the interesting stuff, like is the universe we live in really infinite? But my kindergarten teacher, Mrs. Smith, didn't know the answer to this. She just wanted me to do phonics all the time, even though I already knew how to read. And when I corrected the answers to the math problems she'd left on the board at lunchtime for the Year Six Math Club, the principal told Mom and Dad that I needed to move to another class.

That's how I ended up in Lily's class when I was only six years old. Everyone else in the class was ten or eleven, and they all looked so big to me. The class teacher, Mrs. James, sat me next to Lily so I wouldn't be scared, but I had to take my own cushion to sit on to help me reach the desk.

At first the other kids thought it was funny to have Lily's little sister show up in their class to do science and math. Some of them even called me Baby Brains. I learned about algebra and geometry, evolution and the theory of gravity.

For a while, it was really fun getting to do all these experiments, like making rainbows and building shadow clocks. But then I kept getting the top score on all the class tests, and the names that they called me started to change. Geek. Robot. Freak. And they're just the ones I can tell you about. Never in front of the teacher, but loud enough for me to hear.

I thought Lily would stick up for me, but she didn't say a word. She just sat there with a scowl on her face as I tried my hardest not to cry.

In the end, I couldn't keep it a secret. I told Mom and Dad all about what was happening and said I didn't want to go to school anymore. At first Dad shouted at Lily for not looking after me, but then Lily burst into tears too and said I was ruining her life.

So that's why Mom and Dad decided to teach me at home.

With help from a charity for academically gifted children, they got me this amazing tutor named Mrs. Bradbury. Mrs. Bradbury's really ancient—I think she's over sixty now—but she knows so much about math and science. Before she retired and became my tutor, Mrs. Bradbury used to work for NASA. She was in charge of designing their space probes and satellites, so she had answers to all my questions about how the universe works. Well, most of them, anyway.

When I asked Mrs. Bradbury if the universe was infinite, she told me that scientists just don't know. She explained that we can see only the part of the universe whose light has had the chance to reach us in the fourteen billion years since the Big Bang. This part of the universe measures ninety-three billion light-years across and contains trillions of galaxies, but the whole universe is much, much bigger than this.

Mrs. Bradbury said that some scientists think we live in an infinite universe that stretches on forever in every direction, but other scientists believe that the universe might be shaped like a weird four-dimensional doughnut and this just makes it look like it's infinite.

With the final pole slotted into place, Dad now starts to drag the white canvas material across the roof of the gazebo. As I help him, I catch sight of a tiny ant crawling across the canvas. This ant is scurrying in a straight line, desperately trying to find the edge of the material so it can escape safely onto the grass, but as the canvas is stretched tight into position around the raised center pole, the ant's path starts to circle back on itself.

I watch as the ant crawls blindly on. The roof of the gazebo is curved, so if the ant carries on scurrying in the same direction, it will never reach the edge, just eventually end up back at the same point where it started. For this ant, the gazebo will seem infinitely big, even though it cost only ten dollars from Target.

"What do you think?" Dad asks, stepping back to admire our handiwork.

The gazebo roof rests proudly on the lawn. Reaching across the canvas, I let the ant crawl onto my hand before transporting it safely back onto the grass. As it scurries off into the flower bed, I climb back to my feet.

"It's perfect," I say. "Especially if you're only a few inches tall."

Dad laughs.

"Don't be smart," he says with a grin. "Let's get the legs attached so we can all fit underneath."

But before I can reach for the instructions again, I hear Mom's voice calling me from the kitchen.

"Maisie, phone!"

Breathing hard, I slump with my back against the door, praying that it stays slammed shut.

The air buzzes with silence.

I've still got my eyes tightly closed. I don't even know what I'll see when I open them again. I'm almost too scared to find out.

But a sharp jabbing pain in the palm of my hand forces them open anyway.

The first thing I see is the flat-screen TV in the corner of the room. It looks like it's turned off—there's no picture on the screen, just a faint reflection of the sofa on the other side of the living room. But my gaze instantly drops to focus instead on the source of the pain.

My left hand is clenched into a fist, but as I open it I see the birthday button, its safety pin sticking hard into my skin.

Wincing, I pull the button free. A fresh tear of blood wells up from the tiny hole it leaves behind.

My reality check is still working.

Wiping the blood away with shaking fingers, I pin the button to my pajama top.

If things keep getting strange, I'm going to need this again.

Climbing to my feet, I cautiously look around the room, my heart still thudding in my chest.

The door behind me that leads to the kitchen is closed, but I don't even know if the kitchen is on the other side of it anymore. I saw those blobs of impossible blackness devour everything, a relentless tide of darkness peeling the kitchen inside out as it stretched to fill the universe. My stomach twists as I remember teetering on the edge of this endless void. It was like I was trapped at the beginning and end of everything.

A shudder runs through me. I still don't know how I escaped.

Around the doorframe there's no crack to let the darkness through. It looks like I'm safe—for now. But I need to find out what's happening, fast.

My gaze roams around the living room, desperately searching for any kind of clue. I can see the L-shaped sofa crammed against the wall, the worn leather now more light gray than off-white. Mom's ornaments and photos on the mantelpiece, the bookcase in the corner—a shelf each for Mom, Dad, Lily, and me. Everything seems normal. But when I look through the window, I know this is a lie.

Through the net curtains, I can see the sun shining down on the street outside, cars parked in front of the terraced houses, and above them a clear blue sky. But then my brain fills in what's missing. No people walking past. No Mr. Ferguson next door giving his car its usual Saturday-morning shine. Nobody at all. Everyone's gone. Just like here.

What's on the other side of that window isn't my street. It's an abyss.

I can't stop myself from crying, the tears coming in shuddering gasps that make my whole body shake.

Where's Mom? Where's Dad? Where's Lily?

Where on earth is the world?

The observable universe is supposed to be ninety-three billion light-years wide, but mine has shrunk to the size of this house. And it's getting smaller all the time.

Wiping my eyes with the sleeve of my robe, I try to pull myself together.

Mrs. Bradbury once told me that a good scientist

needs to ask only two questions about the universe: What exists and what does it do? She said if you can answer these questions, you have the chance of understanding everything.

That's what I've got to do now.

At the moment, my universe is everything in this room. So what exists and what does it do?

Picking up the remote control from the corner of the sofa, I switch on the TV. A zero and a one appear in the top right corner of the display, but instead of the news, all I see is the same blank screen as when the TV was turned off. Frustrated, I flick through the channels, but every one's the same. No Saturday-morning cartoons, no celebrity chefs. No picture. No sound. Wherever I am in the universe, there's no signal coming through.

Then the TV crackles, a sudden burst of static that makes me jump in surprise. As the white snow clears from the screen, I see the picture has changed from black to a deep sky blue. My eyes stay glued to the screen as I watch a red balloon float up into this clear blue sky.

Inside my head, I feel a strange sensation, like that feeling you get when you think you've seen something before.

The helium balloon is getting smaller now, dwindling to a red teardrop as it rises higher in the sky.

This is important, but I don't know why.

Then the picture on the TV flickers, the blue sky suddenly fading to black. I press the button on the remote to try to get the picture back, but the screen stays blank. I jab it again, then start pressing every button on the remote, but none of them seems to work anymore. All I can see now is my own reflection on the screen, its shiny blackness reminding me with a shiver of the impossible darkness next door.

Deflated, I sink into the sofa, feeling the leather squeak as gravity pulls me down.

I know I've seen that red balloon before. I remember watching it float up into the same blue sky. It was as if a scene from my memory were playing on the TV, but as I try to remember when it happened, my mind goes blank, just like the TV screen.

On the mantelpiece there's a photo of Mom, Dad, Lily, and me. It was taken a couple of years ago when we went on a family camping trip. It poured the whole week we were away, but this picture was taken in the five minutes of sunshine that we had. In the photo, we're all wearing our raincoats, the camera propped up on a rock as we huddled together for warmth. It was the worst vacation ever, but in the picture we're all laughing, even Lily, because Dad shouted out, "Say freeze!" just before the camera clicked.

This is my family and I want them back.

I can feel my eyes starting to leak again. Looking around for a box of tissues, I notice instead the phone sitting in its stand on the corner table. As I stare at it, Mrs. Bradbury's questions echo again in my mind. *What exists and what does it do?* The TV might just be showing me weird pictures of a red balloon before turning blank, but with this phone I might be able to talk to someone.

Reaching past the figurine of the blue glass cat that stands guard on the table, I pick up the handset. I'm praying that it's not going to be dead just like the TV is now, but when I hold the phone to my ear, I hear a dial tone that tells me it's connected.

The only question is, Who do I call?

My first thought is to call 911. I mean, this is an emergency, isn't it?

But then I think about what I would say if anyone answered the call. *My name is Maisie Day, and I live at Twelve Station Road. My family has disappeared and my house is floating in an endless void that has just erased the kitchen.* Which of the emergency services is going to be able to deal with that?

If I want to find out where my family has gone, that's who I'm going to have to call. My family.

Pushing down the call button, I quickly tap out the number of Mom's phone.

"Come on, come on," I mutter as I wait for the call to connect.

But instead of a ringing tone, I just hear the sound of a click, and then an automated voice says, *"The person you have called is not available at the moment. Please leave a message after the tone."*

BEEP.

"Mom, it's me—Maisie," I splutter, unable to stop myself from crying as the words come tumbling out. "Where are you? Where's everyone? I need you to come and get—"

But before I can finish speaking, the phone cuts off with a dial tone.

Pressing the call button again, I now frantically tap out Dad's number, only to be greeted by the same automated voice.

"The person you have called is not available at the moment. Please leave a message after the tone."

I can't stop myself from screaming.

Nobody's going to answer my call. Nobody's coming to rescue me. I'm trapped here—wherever *here* is—with no way out.

There's only one person left to try. With shaking fingers, I tap out the last number I know by heart.

As the tears run down my face, I wait for the same voice-mail message to kick in again, but instead I hear a ringing tone.

I can't believe it. I cradle the phone against my ear, praying that someone will pick up the call.

Then the ringing tone stops, and I hear my sister's voice on the other end of the line.

"Hello?"

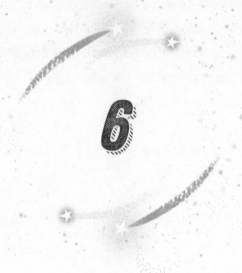

"And you tell that sister of yours to give me a call."
Grandma's voice sounds grumpy on the other end
of the line. "I shouldn't have to wait until dinner to talk
to my granddaughters."

It might be morning here, but for Grandma Pegg it's
dinnertime. That's because she lives in Australia. She
moved there when I was just a baby, so I've seen her in
real life only a couple of times. It costs a lot of money to
fly to Australia.

We went there on vacation once, when I was six, but I
don't remember much about that now. Just the kangaroos
and koalas I saw when Grandma Pegg took me to the zoo.

I speak to Grandma most weekends, though, because she's always calling Mom up to moan about how you can't buy proper peanut butter in the shops and how big the bugs are over there. Once she called in hysterics after she found a funnel-web spider hiding in her underpants when she hung them out on the line.

Dad said he felt sorry for the spider. Mom hit him then.

Mom's always trying to get Grandma Pegg to use her computer to give us a call, but she says she doesn't do technology.

"Are you still there, Lily?" Grandma's voice echoes slightly as it bounces off the satellite to reach me here.

"I'm here, Grandma. And it's me—Maisie."

"Good girl. And how are you doing at school?"

Grandma forgets that I don't go to school anymore. She gets me and Lily mixed up too. She gets a lot of things mixed up. I think that's why Mom wants her to come back home to live with us.

"Fine," I say. It's quicker than reminding her that I'm studying for an online degree in mathematics and physics. She was so proud when I was the youngest person ever to pass my A-levels, but I think she's forgotten that now.

"You keep working hard and don't forget to send me a picture from your birthday party."

"I will, Grandma."

"Bye, Maisie."

"Bye, Nan."

As I place the phone back in the stand, my arm brushes against the statue of the cat on the corner table. For a second, the blue glass figurine wobbles dangerously, and I have to quickly catch hold of it to stop it from falling to the floor.

I breathe a sigh of relief. That was close. Mom collects these little cat statues, and this one is her favorite. I remember when she told the story about when she got this cat. It's vintage Murano glass, apparently. Mom would kill me if I broke it.

Carefully placing the cat back on the table, I turn around. Through the door to the kitchen I can hear Mom clattering about, the fresh smell of baking making me feel hungry again, even though I've only just eaten breakfast. I glance at my watch. Still over two hours to go before people start arriving for my birthday party and I get the chance to open my presents.

Albert Einstein once said that if you put your hand on a hot stove for a minute it seems like an hour, but if you sit with a pretty girl for an hour it seems like a minute. That's relativity. And a bit sexist, I think. But waiting for my party to get started makes me feel like I'm traveling near the speed of light.

This is because Einstein's special theory of relativity

52

says that time passes slower for someone traveling near the speed of light relative to—that means compared to—someone standing still. The speed of light always stays the same—186,282 miles per second—but time and space can change, depending on where you're looking from. So if I took off in a spaceship from Earth and then zoomed around the galaxy at nearly the speed of light to kill a couple of hours before my birthday party, time would slow down for me compared to everyone back on Earth. Onboard the spaceship, I wouldn't feel like time had slowed down, I'd just think the trip was taking me only a couple of hours, but when I got back to Earth ready to get the party started, I'd discover that decades had passed. All my family would be fifty years older—Lily would be an old lady, and Mom and Dad might even have died.

Shaking my head to try to escape this scary thought, I head for the stairs. If Mom and Dad are busy getting things ready for my party and Lily's disappeared as per usual, I'll just hang out on my own in my room.

From the doorway, my bedroom looks pretty normal: bed, desk, wardrobe, and bookshelves, the color scheme a tasteful lilac and gray. But underneath my cabin bed things get really interesting. That's where I keep my experiments.

Pulling back the checkered bedspread that hangs over the arched entrance, I climb beneath my bed. It's like the TARDIS under here: not exactly bigger than it looks from the outside but definitely full of surprises. Squeezing past the innards of an old-fashioned TV that I've left just inside the entrance, I switch on the lamp so I can inspect my latest experiment.

I'm using this TV to build my own particle accelerator. That's a machine that can speed up and smash subatomic particles. The biggest particle accelerator in the world is called the Large Hadron Collider. It's a seventeen-mile ring of superconducting magnets and cost $4.75 billion to build. Scientists are using this particle accelerator to search for the secrets of the universe, but I'm building my own using this secondhand TV that Dad bought me off eBay for ninety-nine cents.

As he struggled up the stairs with the bulky TV, Dad asked me why I couldn't have got a flat-screen instead. I told him that I needed the cathode ray tube inside the TV, and you don't get those in a flat-screen. Inside the cathode-ray tube, you've got this wire that when it gets heated up spits out tiny subatomic particles called electrons. These electrons are then accelerated in a beam before being deflected by a series of magnetic coils until they hit the back of the TV screen. The back of the screen is coated in stuff called phosphor, which glows when the electrons hit, and it's these tiny spots of glowing color that make up the picture you see on the TV.

I turn what's left of the TV on. As it hums to life, I closely watch the screen. Instead of *Scooby-Doo* I see a white spot in the center of the screen. This is the beam of electrons.

Reaching behind me, I grab hold of my shoebox of scientific equipment. Ignoring the Geiger counter resting on the top, I rummage around inside the box until I find what I'm looking for.

Bringing the magnet toward the side of the tube, I watch the white spot on the screen zip upward. Then, as I pull the magnet away, the spot returns to the center of the screen. It works. The magnet is bending the path of the electron beam.

I close my eyes, trying to visualize what's happening. Nearly two hundred years ago a scientist named Michael Faraday showed that there are invisible spiderwebs called fields that fill the universe. When I bring the magnet toward the TV, the strands of these invisible webs mingle and cause the electrons to curve toward the edge of the screen.

I imagine these gossamer-thin lines stretching in every direction, trembling in response to the slightest disturbance in the universe. I open my eyes. Even light is just the rippling of this spiderweb as it stretches through space.

I turn off the TV with a sigh. I thought that being ten

would feel different, but so far it's just the same. Me stuck in my room thinking about science while Lily ignores me from upstairs.

If space *is* infinite, Mrs. Bradbury says this means there's another galaxy out there that looks just like ours. This is because there are only so many ways that atoms can be arranged to make stars, planets, people, and stuff, so in an infinite universe things would just keep on getting repeated, but randomly. In an infinite universe, there's an infinite number of Maisies out there, just like me.

I bet they're having a more interesting birthday.

Outside my bedroom, I hear the clattering sound of Lily's footsteps coming down the stairs. I sit tight in my Batcave, waiting to see if she's coming to say sorry for being such a pain on my birthday. But instead of a knock on my bedroom door, I hear the bathroom door slam shut.

Lily never apologizes.

Climbing out from under the cabin bed, I walk across and open my bedroom door. Across the landing I can see the closed bathroom door. I hover in the doorway, trying to decide what to do.

Maybe if I accidentally bump into Lily when she comes out of the bathroom, she'll do something with me. It is my birthday, after all. We could play a video game together, or maybe just go out in the garden and giggle at Dad making a mess of putting up the gazebo, or even—

From inside the bathroom I hear the sound of Lily crying.

For a second, I'm not 100 percent sure that's what I've heard, but then I hear another long, shuddering sob, followed by the sound of Lily's voice, barely louder than a whisper.

"Oh God . . ."

Suddenly worried, I gently knock on the bathroom door.

"Lily? Are you okay?"

No answer.

Downstairs I hear the distant whirr of a food blender as Mom carries on baking up a storm, but inside the bathroom there's just silence now.

"Lily?" I ask again, knocking a little louder as I put my ear to the door. "Do you want me to get Mom?"

That's when the bathroom door opens and Lily stares back at me, dark circles beneath her bloodshot eyes.

I'm just about to ask her again if she's okay when she grabs hold of my T-shirt and drags me inside.

"Lily, is that you? You've got to help me. You won't believe what's happening."

"Maisie?"

The sound of my sister's voice on the end of the telephone line is all echoey and strange.

"Lily, where are you?" I sob, trying hard to stop myself from losing it completely. "When I woke up, there was nobody here. Mom, Dad, you—you'd all left me behind and I don't know what's going on anymore."

On the other end of the line I hear Lily whisper a word that would get her in so much trouble with Mom.

"Things are getting really weird here, Lily. Everything's

gone. The world outside's just disappeared, and all that's left is this darkness. And I think it's coming to get me." Tears stream down my face as the words rush out of me in a torrent. "I don't even know what's real anymore. I'm trapped in this nightmare and I don't know how to get out."

"Maisie." Lily's voice sounds even farther away now, a distorting crackle on the line making me strain to catch what she's saying. "I'm so sorry. I'm going to put things ri—"

A high-pitched electronic whine cuts her words off midsentence, the screeching sound so painful I have to pull the phone away from my ear. Then this electronic whine is cut off too. Quickly I put the phone back to my ear.

"Lily, are you still there?"

There's no reply. Not even a dial tone. Just an empty silence that stretches on forever.

I can't stop myself from sobbing as I press redial.

Please, Lily, come back.

But the line stays dead, not even the sound of an automated voice this time.

With a frustrated howl, I slam the phone back into its base, the impact causing the figurine on the edge of the table to teeter and fall. Realizing my mistake, I lunge forward to try to catch the blue glass cat, its tear-shaped tail pointing upward as it tumbles through space. But I'm too late, and the figurine smashes into pieces as it hits the wood floor.

I stare at the broken statue, tears still running down my face.

This was Mom's favorite. Dad bought it for her from a flea market when they first got married. She says this is what made her start collecting her little glass cats.

And now it's smashed to bits.

I'm in so much trouble.

Then I laugh. It's only a hollow laugh, but the way I'm feeling right now, any kind of laugh seems like a miracle.

With everything that's happening, breaking Mom's favorite figurine is the least of my worries.

On the polished floorboards the broken pieces of glass still seem to be moving, a trembling motion that makes me think for a second that the whole house is shaking. But as I look around, everything else in the room is completely still. It's just these broken pieces of blue glass that can't seem to stop shivering.

With a frightened fascination I watch as the shattered fragments slowly start to piece themselves back together, the chips and shards of glass scattering in reverse as the broken figurine takes shape again.

I can't believe what I'm seeing as the blue glass cat

jumps into the air, rising as swiftly as it fell and landing with a teeter on the table. For a second, it trembles, then stops, the feline figurine miraculously restored.

With a shaking hand I reach out to touch the cat. Its blue glass tail feels smooth to the touch, not a single flaw or crack to be seen. Moments ago this was smashed to pieces on the floor and now it's perfect again.

I don't understand what's happening. First those black blobs erasing the kitchen and now this blue glass cat turning back time. My house has become a palace of impossibility.

Then I remember the time when Lily and I tried to make Mom a birthday cake. It was over the Christmas holidays last year. Mom's birthday is on the twenty-eighth of December, smack dab between Christmas Day and New Year's Eve. Mom always says this is the worst time ever to have a birthday, but it does make it cheaper to buy her a present in the after-Christmas sales.

Anyway, Dad had made sure Mom was safely out of the way, and Lily and I were busy baking in the kitchen. I say we were busy baking, but all we'd done so far was pull almost every ingredient out of the cupboards while we argued about what kind of cake we were going to make. In the end we'd agreed on chocolate, and Lily had started mixing the butter and sugar in a bowl.

I was supposed to be beating the eggs, but I hadn't

even got them out of the fridge. I'd got distracted by this book Mrs. Bradbury had given me for Christmas. It was called *A Brief History of Time* by Stephen Hawking. With a title like that, I'd thought it was going to be some completely boring book about the history of clocks, but it was actually all about the Big Bang, black holes, and how the universe works. It was the best book I'd ever read.

I was leaning against the fridge with my head stuck in chapter seven, reading about entropy and the arrow of time, when the sound of Lily's voice pulled me out of its pages.

"Maisie!"

I looked up to see Lily standing by the mixing bowl with a scowl on her face.

"What?"

"The eggs," she said with a theatrical sigh.

She sounded really annoyed at me already, and we'd only just started making the cake. Dad had said it would be nice for us to do something together for Mom, but I didn't think it was going to be much fun if Lily was just going to order me around.

Reaching inside the fridge, I pulled out a carton of eggs. My brain was still buzzing with the part of the book I'd just been reading, and as I looked at the egg carton, an idea jumped into my head. A way I could finally make Lily understand how totally amazing science is. Opening the carton, I took out an egg, but as Lily held out her hand for it, I asked her a question instead.

"What's this egg made of?"

Lily looked at me as if I was stupid.

"It's an egg, Maisie. It's made out of egg."

I shook my head.

"No, you don't understand," I said, ignoring the look of irritation on her face. "It's made out of atoms. Everything's made out of atoms. But in this egg, all the atoms are arranged in a particular way."

Then I dropped the egg.

Lily gasped in shock as it smashed on the floor.

"Maisie!"

"Don't worry," I quickly said, looking down at the yolky mess. Broken shards of eggshell were now scattered across the floor. "I'll clean it up. But take a look at the egg, Lily. What's it made of now?"

Lily sighed, just like she always does whenever I try to get her interested in science.

"Atoms," she said, her voice a dull monotone. "It's still made out of atoms."

"Exactly," I replied, feeling excited that Lily understood. "It's made of exactly the same atoms as before, but they're arranged *differently* now."

"Yeah," Lily said. "It's broken, and now you're going to have to clean it up."

"I know," I said. "But there were so many different ways in which the egg could break. When the egg was whole, its atoms were arranged in a highly organized way, but now they're just disorganized and random. The *entropy* of the egg has increased."

Lily frowned as she stared at the eggy mess that was splattered on the floor. "What's *entropy*?"

"Entropy is how random and disordered something is," I said excitedly. "In the universe, entropy is always increasing. Eggs break, glasses smash, stars burn themselves out. We never see the broken bits of eggshell stick themselves together again to form a perfect egg. There's nothing in the laws of science to say this can't happen, but the chances that each atom could arrange itself in the exact same position as before are so infinitesimally small, you'd probably have to wait until the universe ends before you saw that happen."

I stood there grinning as I waited for Lily to realize how amazing this is, but my sister just shook her head.

"The universe is going to end before we finish making this cake if you keep on dropping the eggs. Stop messing about, Maisie, and clean up this mess."

Lily's words echo in my mind as I sit on the sofa in the empty living room. I stare at the blue glass figurine, the crystal cat now restored to perfection.

The universe must have ended.

That's why I'm on my own.

An unstoppable wave of anger and rage rises inside me. I won't let this happen. I want the universe back in the right place. I want a world that obeys the rules.

I want my family back.

With a flailing hand, I sweep the cat off the table.

The figurine falls, tumbling through the air until it hits the floor and smashes into pieces again. This time, I don't give it a second chance. Picking up the remote control from the sofa, I bring it down on the broken pieces of glass again and again and again. I feel my fingers cut as I pound the splintered shards into dust, the sharp stabs of pain proving to me that this is real, even though I don't want it to be.

The remote control finally slips from my hand, my anger leaving me breathless as I stare down at the shattered figurine. You can't even tell it was a cat anymore; the blue splinters of glass are scattered like fractals across the floor.

I want Mom to run into the room right now to see what I've done—to shout at me, to scream at me. I wouldn't even care if she hit me for smashing up her crystal cat. I just want to see her again.

Still sobbing, I climb slowly to my feet, but then, through my tears, I see my very worst fear.

The TV screen is still blank, but this blackness now

looks much darker than before—the same darkness I first saw when I opened the front door. And it's getting bigger.

I back away, the broken glass crunching beneath my bare feet, but I don't even feel it as I stare spellbound at the screen.

Our TV has only a thirty-two-inch display—Lily's always moaning at Mom and Dad to get a bigger one—but this growing rectangle of darkness must be at least twice that size now. It's as though the living room wall were turning into an indoor movie screen and it's showing the scariest movie I've ever seen.

The bookcase in the corner, the pictures on the mantelpiece, even the mantelpiece itself—everything is being erased by this absolute blackness. And then it starts moving toward me.

It's difficult to tell this at first. The creeping darkness is almost two-dimensional as the walls start to slowly fold in on themselves. I stare at this impossibility, an abyss now gaping on every side of me. I'm trapped—just like the photons of light lost in the Vantablack. And as the darkness reaches out, I know that if it touches me, I'll be lost too.

Spinning around, I see the only sliver of reality that's left—the door that leads to the hall. Desperately I lunge toward it, shoving the door open with a bang as I skid out into the hallway. My bare feet slip on the polished floorboards as I scramble forward, trying to put as much space as possible between myself and this onrushing tide of emptiness as it washes reality away.

As I reach the bottom of the stairs I glance toward the front door, praying that it stays shut. In the tinted-glass arch at the top, each segment of glass is now stained black. It's almost like the house doesn't have to pretend anymore. There's no way I can stop it. The outside is coming in.

I scramble up the stairs, the darkness now lapping at my heels. My heart is pounding in my chest, every snatched breath a desperate prayer that I'll make it to the top. There's nowhere else left to go.

I'm almost there, the top of the stairs a single step away. I can see that the bathroom door is open, the polished white tiles inside a stark contrast to the absolute blackness that's behind me.

I can't stop myself from looking back over my shoulder, just to make sure that I'm safe. And that's when I slip, the trailing hem of my robe snagging on the broken carpet runner that Mom's been nagging Dad to get fixed.

I hit the landing with a thump. Winded, I glance back to see flecks of black foam only a few inches away. The stairs are gone—all that's left is an empty void that stretches on forever.

I don't even have time to get to my feet.

Lunging forward, I scramble across the landing, feeling the cold shock of the porcelain tiles beneath my hands and feet as I reach the bathroom. The infinite darkness surges behind me, erasing the space where I was only seconds before. I kick out with my last ounce of strength, my foot connecting to slam the bathroom door as I collapse sobbing on the floor.

"Lily—get off me!"

Dragging me by my T-shirt, Lily dumps me down on the toilet seat. Luckily, the lid is already pulled down, so it's not as embarrassing as it could be, but I still don't know what I've done to upset my big sister as she glares down at me.

"What's the matter with you?" I ask, smoothing down the sequined star on the front of my top to get rid of the marks where Lily grabbed it. Then I look at my sister again. "Are you okay?"

Lily's face is pale and drawn, dark shadows etched beneath her eyes where her mascara has run. She's still wearing Dad's long-sleeve T-shirt, and beneath his black bird's-nest hair, the pop star on the front has the same panda eyes.

I know I shouldn't say it, but I can't stop the words from escaping from my lips.

"You're a mess."

"Shut up," Lily snaps, and I shrink back on the toilet seat, hugging my arms tight to my chest to protect myself from my sister's fury. She really hates me, I can tell. Fighting hard to stop myself from crying, I blink back my own tears. Why's she being so mean to me?

"It's not fair. You can't tell me to shut up," I protest. "It's my birthday. I'm going to tell Mom and Dad."

Lily laughs hollowly.

"That's your answer to everything, isn't it?" she says with a sneer. "Tell Mom and Dad and expect everything to work out perfectly, like one of your stupid experiments. Just like when you got them to take you out of school and give you a private tutor, while I got left behind. Well, real life's not like one of your experiments, Maisie. Real life is messy and painful and it's not fair."

Lily's spitting her words out now, and I shrink back even farther on the toilet seat.

"You don't know what it's like, Maisie. Everything is so easy for you. You just get to stay here safely at home while I go out into the real world. I'm the one who has

70

Sophie criticizing every fashion choice I make. I'm the one who has Mom and Dad on my back the whole time, nagging me to study. I'm the one who's messed up my entire life. Not you."

Lily's doing it again. Making everything about her. But what about me? I've had enough of staying quiet. I'm ten years old now. It's time Lily listened to me.

"Least you get to have a life," I yell, making Lily lean back in surprise. "Mom and Dad never let me go anywhere on my own. I'm stuck in this house nearly every day, while you get to go to school. It's not my fault I'm good at science and math; I just like the way they help me understand the universe. But they'll never help me understand why you hate me so much!"

Lily stares at me, her mouth open wide in shock at my sudden outburst. Then she slowly shakes her head.

"I don't hate you, Maisie," she says quietly, her eyes shining brightly with the same tears that are now creeping out of mine. "I just wish I could be more like you."

Now it's my turn to look shocked.

"But why would you want to be like me?" I ask, unable to understand why Lily would say something so ridiculous. "You're the popular one—I'm the freak. You've got friends; you get to go out on your own and stay up late. And you're beautiful too."

Sitting down on the edge of the bath, Lily bows her

head. She's fiddling with the hem of her sleeve, stretching the material almost to breaking point as she pulls it down over her wrist.

"I'm not beautiful," she says, shaking her head scornfully as she lets the sleeve hang. "I'm disfigured."

I feel really confused. I don't know why Lily is saying this. She's not disfigured. She's really pretty. Without thinking, I reach out for Lily's hand, just wanting to let my sister know that she's talking nonsense.

But as I reach for her hand my fingers catch on the hem of her sleeve, revealing a strange black mark on the inside of Lily's wrist.

Lily snatches her hand away, but it's too late. I've seen it. "Is that a tattoo?"

A tsunami of emotions washes across Lily's face—anger, fear, disgust, shame. Then she slowly nods.

"We were all supposed to get one," Lily says, her voice trembling slightly. "Sophie, Daisy, Lauren, and me. We'd spent forever choosing a design and even got fake IDs so we looked old enough. I went first, but then when I had mine done, Sophie took one look at it and said it looked tacky. She changed her mind and told the others not to bother either. So now I'm the only one who's got a tattoo." Lily looks down at her wrist, her face screwed up in disgust. "It means eternity, and now I'm stuck with it forever."

I can't stop myself from looking at my sister's tattoo, her pale skin now marked with this black loop of ink.

"It's a Möbius strip," I say.

"What do you mean?" Lily asks, her forehead furrowing into a frown. "What's a Möbius strip?"

I remember asking Mrs. Bradbury the same question when she was teaching me hyperbolic geometry.

"It's like the scientific symbol for infinity," I reply. "A Möbius strip is an infinite loop that you can never escape from."

Lily's face crumples.

"You're telling me that I've got a science tattoo?"

Then she really starts to cry, her whole body shaking as her words come out in shuddering gasps.

"Mom and Dad are going to kill me when they see it," she sobs. "It's the middle of summer and I can't even wear anything with short sleeves in case they spot it. I don't know what I'm going to do!"

I've never seen Lily this upset before. Part of me just wants to run downstairs to get Mom, but I know that would be completely the wrong thing to do. I stare at the infinite loop tattooed on the inside of her wrist, racking my brain for something helpful to say that will stop my sister's crying.

"Why don't you just put a Band-Aid on it?"

Lily looks up at me, the mascara smudges beneath her eyes making her look like a doubting panda.

"You could say a cat scratched you or something," I explain. "It'll give you an excuse to keep the tattoo covered up while we work out what to do."

I don't know what Lily's going to say. Call me stupid. Shout at me. Scream in my face. But instead I see a faint hopeful smile start to creep across her lips.

"That might work," she says. "Maisie, you're a genius."

I feel my cheeks flush. I might be academically gifted, but Lily's never said anything like this to me before.

"But you've got to promise not to tell Mom and Dad," she continues, wiping her tears with her sleeve. "I couldn't face them ranting about how I'll never be able to get a job with a tattoo and how I'll regret it when I get older." She glances again at the black loop of ink on her wrist. "I regret it already."

Looking up, Lily meets my gaze with a pleading stare.

"Do you understand?"

Pythagoras said that the number ten contains the key to understanding everything. I think he was right. Now that I'm ten, Lily's speaking to me like I'm a grown-up. And I *do* understand.

I nod.

"I won't tell Mom and Dad."

"Thanks, Maisie," Lily says, the muscles around her

lips finally remembering how to smile for real. "I owe you one."

"Lily!"

A look of panic flashes across Lily's face as Mom's voice echoes up the stairs. Reaching for her wrist, she tugs at her sleeve to hide the tattoo.

"I'll go," I say, springing up off the toilet. "I can keep Mom busy while you wash your face and put a Band-Aid on."

Pulling the bathroom door open, I head across the landing. Behind me I hear Lily opening the cabinet where Mom keeps the Band-Aids as I bounce down the stairs.

Inside, I feel the same surge of excitement I felt when I woke up this morning. But it's not because it's my birthday. It's because I feel like I've got my sister back.

S itting on the toilet seat, I stare blankly at the bath-room door. My knees are pulled up to my chest with my arms wrapped tightly around them, but this doesn't make me feel any safer. The door might be closed, but I know what's waiting for me on the other side.

I'm counting every breath I take as my heartbeat grad-ually slows to something nearing normality. If I focus on this, maybe it will stop me from falling apart.

Everything's gone. I watched that tide of absolute darkness devouring everything in its path. The kitchen, the living room, the hallway, and the stairs—I guess all that's left now is this bathroom I'm sitting in, and I don't know how much longer this will last.

When she first started teaching me, Mrs. Bradbury asked what I liked best about science. I told her I liked science because it helped me understand the universe, but nothing I've learned in science can help me make sense of anything that's happening now. I remember the flecks of nothingness, foaming on the edge of that impossible abyss. Infinite. Unknowable.

Then I remember what Mrs. Bradbury said next.

"Science can't help you understand everything, Maisie." Taking off her glasses, Mrs. Bradbury started to polish the lenses with the sleeve of her cardigan. "There's so much we still don't know."

Holding up her glasses to the light to check for smears, Mrs. Bradbury then placed them back on her face, peering through the lenses at the textbook open on the table between us. She pointed down at the contents page, running her finger along the list of topics covered in the book.

"I can teach you how the chemical elements formed and about the structure of an atom. We'll cover electromagnetism, radioactivity, and the quantum of light. You'll learn why Earth orbits the sun, how the sun orbits the Milky Way, and why the Milky Way will eventually collide with the distant galaxy of Andromeda, billions of years from now. But everything that science has seen or ever observed, from the smallest subatomic particle to the most distant star, makes up less than five percent of the universe. The rest is completely unknown."

I remember scratching my head as I tried to work this out. I stared through the patio doors at a darkening sky, faint pinpricks of white studding the blue as the stars slowly came out.

"That's impossible," I said. "You told me there were billions of stars in the Milky Way, and the Milky Way is only one of the trillions of galaxies that exist. How can all that add up to just five percent of the universe?"

"Less than five percent," Mrs. Bradbury corrected me. "You see, the visible universe—all the stars, planets, comets, everything on Earth, even us—is all made out of ordinary matter. But nearly a quarter of the universe seems to be made of a mysterious substance that scientists can't even detect. We call this dark matter, but what it is, we just don't know. And the rest of the universe seems to consist of a mysterious force called dark energy, which might eventually tear our universe apart."

Behind her glasses, wrinkles furrowed around my tutor's eyes as her features creased into an encouraging smile.

"Maybe you'll be the first person to discover what this really is, Maisie, and expand our knowledge of the universe, but don't be in so much of a hurry to understand everything that you miss out on the fun of being young."

Beneath my pajama bottoms, the toilet seat feels freezing cold. I'm ten years old today and this isn't any fun.

Maybe the impossible darkness that's destroying my home is dark matter, or it could be dark energy, but what does it matter if I discover what it is, if there's nobody left in the universe to tell?

In the living room just now I managed to speak to Lily on the phone. Only for a few seconds, but that was enough to prove I'm not completely alone. There must be something out there apart from that infinite emptiness. And maybe Lily can help me to find a way out of this nightmare. . . .

I run over her words in my mind. *"I'm so sorry. I'm going to put things ri—"* Lily's sentence was cut off midflow, but it must mean something. Why did she say she was sorry? And how can she possibly put things right?

I glance around the bathroom. From my position perched on top of the toilet, I can see the sink and the bathroom cabinet, the laundry basket in the corner and the towels folded over the towel rail. Blue for Dad, green for Mom, purple for Lily, and yellow for me. Above the bath, the white metal slats of the blinds are shut tight against the darkness outside.

Nobody's bathroom has a clock in it, but ours does. Dad put it up after Lily kept hogging the bathroom every morning when she was supposed to be getting ready for school. Mom, Dad, and I would be waiting outside while Lily spent two hours in the shower. Dad says she's got no excuse now for not knowing how long she's been in here.

I look at the time on the clock.

The hour and minute hands stand at a perfect right angle, telling me it's nine o'clock.

That's not right.

It was nine o'clock when I woke up this morning. I remember the time flashing on my alarm clock. And so much has happened since then. This clock must have stopped, I think—maybe the batteries have run out—but looking more closely, I see the second hand tremble before ticking forward a single second.

It must be running slow, then, the last bit of battery juice stretching out the seconds into hours.

I shiver. The bathroom suddenly feels cold, the shadows cast by the light overhead starting to lengthen across the white-tiled floor.

Wait a second. How can that even be possible? When you're outside, shadows change shape due to the position of the sun. When the sun's high in the sky, your shadow is short, but when the sun's low, your shadow gets longer as you block out more of the sun's light. But the bathroom light overhead isn't moving, is it?

I glance up and discover that things have taken a turn for the weird again.

Tiny specks of dust are dancing in the light spilling

down from the ceiling, twisting in shifting patterns as the dust particles are bombarded by invisible molecules of air. But seeing Einstein's theory of Brownian motion in action isn't what makes me gasp in surprise. It's the fact that the light beams are curving downward.

It's like when you pull the plug out of the bath and the water swirls around, taking your rubber duck on a crazy trip around the drain as the bath slowly empties. That's what's happening here, but instead of water, it's the light that seems to be swirling around, the beams curling as they loop on seemingly endless paths around the bathroom.

My head hurts as I try to make sense of this impossibility. That's why the shadows are lengthening. This light isn't coming from straight overhead but is hitting things almost sideways, casting long shadows in every direction. The white tiles covering the floor are shrouded in darkness now, and I'm almost afraid to step on them in case this is something to do with the emptiness outside.

But I've got to find out what's happening here.

Climbing down off the toilet, I grab hold of the edge of the sink, clinging to it to keep myself upright as the bathroom seems to spin like a fairground ride. I can see my reflection in the mirror, wide-open eyes staring in fear as strange shadows fall across my face. A wave of nausea rises inside me, and it's all I can do to stop myself from throwing up in the sink.

Then I watch as my hair slowly rises from my head, fanning out to create a blond halo that frames the look of terror on my face. When Mom and Dad took me to the Museum of Science and Industry, there was this thing called a Van de Graaff generator. It was like a silver globe that you could hold, and when you did, the static electricity it generated made your hair stand on end. Lily couldn't stop laughing at me as my blond shock of hair stuck up in every direction like the worst haircut ever.

But I'm not laughing now. Reaching, I try to brush my hair back down, but it just keeps springing up again. It feels like someone's tugging at the end of each strand, the sensation getting more painful with every second that passes. Then I hear a rattling noise.

Looking down, I see the chipped mug standing on the corner of the sink, our color-coded toothbrushes rattling around inside it. Then I watch astounded as my yellow toothbrush rises into the air, closely followed by the others. Dad's blue toothbrush rotates as it rises, its spin sending a spray of minty-fresh droplets onto my face.

I rub my eyes, still clinging to the sink with one hand as I lift my head to see the objects that are orbiting the room. Above the bath, the showerhead is rising like a snake charmed from its basket, showering me with spray again as it twists toward the ceiling. The towels are being dragged upward too, their primary colors now changing shade as the light seems to stretch around them. Shower gel, shampoo bottles, toilet-paper rolls, and jars of moisturizer—everything is spiraling in ever-decreasing circles toward the same point, a pinprick of dark in the center of the light.

At the supermarket when I was little, Mom always used to let me put her spare change in the money spinner. This was a charity collection box that was shaped like a giant lollipop. I used to lay each coin flat in exactly the right spot on the clear plastic dome, then let go and watch as the quarter swirled around and around the curved track, its circles getting smaller with every orbit, before it finally fell through the central hole into the coin container.

My insides twist as I feel this same falling sensation. I grab hold of the sink with both hands again, trying to resist with every ounce of strength I've got left.

That's what must be happening here. This isn't some invisible force pulling everything to the ceiling, but space itself being curved. That's why Earth orbits the sun—it's just falling in a curving path around the dent in space that's caused by the sun. This is Einstein's theory of gravity. The bigger the object, the bigger the dent and the more space is curved. And gravity doesn't just change the shape of space, but the pace of time as well. That's be-cause Einstein worked out that space and time aren't sep-arate things, but a single thing—space-time. The clock on the wall isn't running slow—it's gravity that's causing time to dilate.

I feel my feet rise from the floor. Looking up, I can see everything stretching around a central sphere of dark-ness, the light beams looping back in a sudden flare of brightness. I can barely hold on anymore.

Only something supermassive could cause space-time to warp like this.

There's something huge above my head.

But there's only one room up there.

Lily's bedroom.

As my fingers start to slip, my mind races to make the connection. Einstein thought that if you could bend space-time enough, you could bring two separate loca-tions together—like folding a piece of paper in half to join the top and the bottom. This creates a wormhole—a tunnel—and Einstein said if you could travel through this wormhole, you could take a shortcut across the uni-verse. Or maybe even take a trip to another universe completely.

The dark sphere hangs suspended, a frozen point in space and time as chaos swirls around it.

I don't know if this is a way out of this nightmare or a

one-way trip to oblivion. I remember that infinite blackness devouring everything in its path and then hear the
echo of Lily's voice whispering in my ear. *I'm so sorry.*

I can't wait for Lily to put things right. I've got to do
this on my own.

Feeling gravity's pull, I lift my head high.

And then I let go.

Swinging into the kitchen, I see Mom bent over a mountain of sandwiches that are piled high on the kitchen table.

"Lily, I need you to get me some paper plates from the store," she begins, trying to balance the last cheese-and-ham triangle on top of Sandwich Mountain. With this in place, she looks up to see me standing in front of the table. "Oh, Maisie, it's you. Where's your sister?"

"She's just getting ready," I say, remembering my promise to Lily.

There's a smudge of cream near the corner of Mom's mouth. The smell of freshly baked cake makes my mouth water.

"You've got something on your face," I tell her, lifting my hand to the corner of my mouth to show Mom where.

With a guilty expression, Mom reaches up to wipe her cheek.

"The other side," I say.

Finding the right place, Mom dabs the cream with her fingers and then licks the evidence away.

"Making all this party food is hungry work," she says with a grin. "Do you think we've got enough?"

I look at the jam-packed plates and bowls laid out like the Himalayas across the table. There are chicken drumsticks and mini-quiches, slices of pizza and sausage rolls, hot dogs, burgers, sandwiches of every description, bowls of chips, and cubes of cheese and pineapple speared on toothpicks. And that's just the savory stuff. On the side I can see cupcakes, meringues, chocolate éclairs, and fruit kebabs.

"Just a bit," I reply with a grin, the excited smile on my face matching Mom's.

I sneak a chip out of the nearest bowl.

"But I need more paper plates," Mom says as I start crunching. "Just to make sure we've got enough for everyone. That's why I want Lily to pop out to the store."

Leaning toward the door, she shouts up the stairs.

"Lily!"

Quickly swallowing my chip, I interrupt Mom before she calls out again.

"Let me go get them."

At this suggestion, Mom's face creases into a frown.

"Don't be silly, Maisie—it's *your* birthday. You can't be running around getting things ready for your own party. Lily can get them for me."

It might be my birthday, but that's not the reason Mom doesn't want me to go to the store. She never lets me go. Not on my own, anyway. The convenience store is only over the railway bridge, halfway down the promenade, but Mom says it's too far for me to go there on my own. I thought things would be different now that I'm ten.

"But I want to go," I say, putting on my best "it's my birthday" face.

Mom still looks doubtful. She glances over her shoulder toward the patio doors. Through the window I can see Dad pegging out the guy ropes, the gazebo now standing upright in the center of the lawn: too busy at the moment to give Mom the backup I know she's waiting for.

"I'm not sure, Maisie," she finally replies. "I think it's better if Lily goes. You see, I want you to help me choose what party games you want to play."

I'm studying for a degree in mathematics and physics at the Open University. I wish Mom would stop treating me like a baby.

"I don't want to play any party games," I snap. "I

want you to let me go to the store on my own. I'm ten years old."

I nearly shout this last part out, and Mom looks really shocked. She's used to Lily blowing her top, but I almost never lose my temper. I just need her to know how important this is to me.

"Please, Mom."

A frown still creases Mom's forehead, but as she looks at me I see the worry lines around her eyes start to soften and, for a second, I think she's going to say yes. But then Lily walks through the door and ruins everything.

"What's up?" she asks.

Lily looks completely different from how I left her in the bathroom. Dad's long-sleeve T-shirt is gone, and instead she's wearing a tie-dyed vest and denim shorts. The dark shadows beneath her eyes are disguised with a layer of concealer, and her pale skin shines like starlight, but I can just glimpse the Band-Aid sticking to the underside of her wrist.

The frown on Mom's face vanishes at Lily's appearance.

"There you are," she says, dusting her hands on the front of her apron and then reaching for her purse on the table. "I need you to pick up some paper plates."

I start to protest, but Mom quickly presses the twenty-dollar bill she's pulled from her purse into my hand.

"And we need some more drinks too. Coke, lemonade, orange juice—you choose. It'll take the two of you to carry it all."

I'm about to start arguing, but Lily just plucks the twenty out of my hand.

"Come on, Maisie," she says, giving me a pointed look. "It'll be fun. We can chat about stuff on the way."

M y mind reels as I spin toward the dark sphere, the size of it growing larger and larger until it almost fills my vision. Everything is spiraling around this black hole in a kaleidoscope of colors, the shapes of things stretched and distorted as they curve around the void. Ahead of me, I see Dad's toothbrush stretched impossibly thin, its color shifting from blue to red as it seems to freeze on the edge of the darkness.

I can feel myself being stretched in the same way, the immense gravity pulling at every atom of my being. It's like I'm being torn apart. All I can see is the darkness now; everything else is a distant blur of distortion at the very edge of my vision.

Things are speeding up.

The dark globe surrounds me now. It's as though I'm inside and outside of it at the same time, the confusion inside my brain stretched to breaking point as I slip over the edge. I'm falling into infinity, and I don't know if I'll ever stop.

And then in the darkness I see a dome of light squeezed into a narrowing point. I'm hurtling toward it, and now this blinding light is all I can see. I'm going to hit—

I close my eyes, waiting for an impact that never comes, and then I open them again to find that everything has changed.

I'm standing on the stairs that lead to Lily's room.

There's no dark globe. There's no point of blinding light. The crushing force I felt pulling me apart is gone.

There are just the stairs that lead to my sister's bedroom. And I'm halfway up.

Einstein's theory of gravity explains the movement of every star and planet in the sky and predicts how wormholes could connect two points in space-time. A bridge across the universe or a shortcut from the bathroom to the stairs. That's the only way I can explain how I'm standing here.

I start to bound up the stairs, desperate to see if Lily's in her room, but as I look up I realize that this nightmare isn't over yet.

At the top of the stairs I can't see the door to Lily's bedroom. In fact, I can't even see the top of the stairs, just an endless sequence of steps stretching on forever.

I freeze, swaying in confusion as a wave of nausea rises up inside me again. Glancing back over my shoulder, I see the same picture in reverse, the steps leading down in a never-ending staircase.

I turn back, fear thumping in my chest as I try to make sense of it all. I start to climb, thinking that this must be some kind of optical illusion—like that picture of an impossible staircase that I saw when Mrs. Bradbury took me to the art gallery.

Most of the time, Mrs. Bradbury taught me at home. We'd sit at the kitchen table with a textbook open between us as we talked about life, the universe, and everything. But sometimes Mrs. Bradbury took me on field trips too.

There was this exhibition at the local gallery by an artist called M. C. Escher, and Mrs. Bradbury thought it would help me with my geometry.

"Escher said he was a 'reality enthusiast,'" Mrs. Bradbury explained as we walked around the gallery. "His art speaks in the language of mathematics and science to show us a picture of the universe."

I think about the pictures we've seen so far—lizards crawling out of jigsaw puzzles, strange patterns of birds and fish, a single eye staring out toward us with a reflection of a skull inside.

"He had a pretty weird view of reality."

Mrs. Bradbury laughed.

"Well, the universe is a pretty weird place," she agreed.

There was a group of schoolchildren standing around the next picture, so we had to wait for them to move on before we could see it. They looked about Lily's age, all wearing the same maroon uniforms, although some of the girls seemed to have found ways of accessorizing to make them look cooler. As their teacher finished talking about the picture and led them on to the next one, calling out to a couple of girls at the back to stop chatting and keep up, I couldn't help feeling jealous of them. I mean, I love learning stuff with Mrs. Bradbury, but sometimes I think being "academically gifted" means I've missed out on the chance to have friends.

"What do you think of this one?" Mrs. Bradbury asked as we stood in front of the picture.

It was a black-and-white drawing of an old-fashioned building, the picture showing a bird's-eye view. My eye was immediately drawn to the central staircase at the top of the building, its steps arranged in the shape of a square. A group of creepy-looking men, all dressed in hoods, were walking up and down, passing each other on the stairs. But as I stared at this scene, my brain started to rebel as I tried to work out what was wrong.

"Where does the staircase go?" I asked. "They're walking up and down at the same time."

Mrs. Bradbury smiled.

"Well done, Maisie. The title of this picture is *Ascending and Descending,* but most people call it the impossible staircase."

Stepping forward, her finger hovered above the surface of the picture, tracing the path of the hooded figures as they climbed the stairs. Each turn seemed to take them higher or lower depending on the direction they were facing, but as Mrs. Bradbury's finger finished tracing the fourth side of the staircase it arrived again at the point she'd started from.

"The staircase is never-ending," she explained. "Nobody will ever reach the top. It's an optical illusion, but Escher based this picture on a shape that was created by a mathematician and a scientist. It's an impossible object—something that can't exist in the three-dimensional world in which we live, but geometry allows us to create shapes in four or more dimensions. We have to use equations to describe these shapes because we can't draw them on paper or model them out of clay. But according to math, they're as real as a triangle or a cube."

Mrs. Bradbury's words echo in my head as my feet pound up the stairs. *Real . . . Impossible . . . Never-ending . . .* I keep climbing, straining my eyes for a glimpse of the top of the stairs, but it never comes.

Panicking, I double-back on myself, desperate to find a way out. My feet thunder down the steps, the same sound I hear every morning when Lily gets out of bed and comes downstairs. But instead of arriving at the landing after a dozen or so steps, the stairs just carry on, step after step after step. I can't stand it.

I remember how, when the kitchen seemed to be expanding around me, all I had to do to escape was close my eyes and turn the door handle. Maybe that's what I've got to do now. If what my eyes are showing me is impossible, then I need to trust my other senses to find a way out.

My hand is shaking as I grab hold of the railing. Closing my eyes, I start to climb again, slower this time, counting every step as I go. *One, two, three, four* . . . If I'm right, I just need to focus on what must be real, the worn fibers of the carpet under my bare feet, the polished railing sliding beneath my hand as I climb. *Eight, nine, ten, eleven* . . . Only a few more steps until I make it to Lily's room.

I remember her voice echoing on the other end of the line. *"I'm so sorry. I'm going to put things ri—"* Lily's words were cut off midsentence, but if I can make it to the top, then maybe I can find Lily and she can keep her promise to me.

But the steps keep on coming. *Fourteen, fifteen, sixteen, seventeen* . . . My footsteps start to falter, the sound of my heart thumping loudly in my chest as I realize what this means. *Nineteen, twenty, twenty-one* . . .

I can't wait any longer.

I open my eyes and my heart breaks in two.

All I can see is an endless sequence of steps rising ahead of me. The stairs go on forever.

Letting go of the railing, I sink to my knees. I can't stop myself from sobbing as a fresh wave of despair overwhelms me.

This is my house. These are the stairs to Lily's room. But I'm never going to get there.

I feel like giving up and rushing down the stairs to surrender to the emptiness that's devoured my home. But I can't even do that anymore, as the stairs stretch endlessly in both directions. I'm going to be trapped here forever.

A fresh wave of sobs shakes my body. All I want is my family back.

Then, through my tears, I glimpse a figure on the step beside me. Glancing up, I see . . . another me. The same lilac robe that I'm wearing, my own face fixed on the stairs straight ahead as I'm frozen in the act of climbing them. And in front of this other Maisie, I see another and another and another, an endless line of Maisies heading in both directions on the stairs.

Each one is frozen in a moment of time and, as I glance back down the stairs, I see more—an infinity of

Maisies climbing up and down. It's as though I'm endlessly ascending and descending—just like the people in that picture at the art gallery.

I reach out toward the Maisie who's closest to me, but my hand just passes straight through her, the figure only visible when it's refracted through my tears.

This doesn't make any sense. How can I be everywhere but stuck going nowhere?

My mind rebels. People can't be in more than one place at the same time, but then my brain reminds me what can.

Everything in the universe is made of tiny particles. The stars in the sky and the molecules inside my body are all made out of atoms. Every atom consists of even smaller particles: protons, neutrons, and electrons. But when these electrons move around, it's impossible for scientists to work out exactly where they are. All they can do is calculate the probability of finding an electron in a specific place.

This is where it gets really weird. To work out the probability of finding the electron in a particular place, scientists have to calculate every possible route it could have taken to get to that precise spot. That's the only way they can get the right answer. It's as though the electron travels by every possible path at the same time.

The electron is *everywhere* at once—just like me.

Through my tears, I stare at the never-ending Maisies climbing up and down the stairs.

But I'm a person—not a subatomic particle.

Choking back another sob, I try to catch my breath. It feels like I'm hyperventilating, my heart pounding in my chest as I try to work out what this means.

Sliding my right hand beneath my robe, I hold it against the center of myself, trying to focus on this one thing to calm my racing heart.

And that's when I notice something really strange.

Your heart sits in the center of your chest, but slightly on the left. But as my heartbeat thuds against my fingers, it feels like mine is on the right. I move my hand from left to right, trying to find the place where my heartbeat feels strongest, and it's definitely on the right.

My heart's in the wrong place.

I can't hold it together anymore, my gulping sobs turning into hysterical laughter. How can my heart be on the wrong side of my body? Just another item to add to my list of impossible things, along with an infinity of Maisies and stairs that never end.

Then I remember another almost impossible object that Mrs. Bradbury showed me when we got back from the art gallery.

"A normal piece of paper has two sides," Mrs. Bradbury said, tearing a strip from the topmost sheet of her pad. She turned this strip of paper over in her hands. "The front and the back. But if I take this strip of paper, give it a twist, and then join the ends together, I've created a Möbius strip."

"What's a Möbius strip?" I asked as I watched my tutor tape the two ends together.

"It resembles the scientific symbol for infinity," she replied. "A Möbius strip is an infinite loop that you can never escape from." Mrs. Bradbury handed me the twisted loop of paper that she'd made. "Find out for yourself. I want you to draw a line down the center of the strip and don't stop until you reach the point you started from."

Feeling a bit puzzled, I picked up my pencil and, resting the Möbius strip on the table, started to draw a line down the center of the strip. As the paper looped around, my pencil followed it, the line I was drawing crossing over the band of tape that Mrs. Bradbury had used to join the ends together not once but twice, before reaching the start of the line again.

"There you go."

I started to hand the strip of paper back to Mrs. Bradbury, but she shook her head.

"Take a closer look," she said. "How many sides does the strip of paper have now?"

I turned the Möbius strip over in my hand. The line that I'd drawn seemed to cover both sides of the twisted loop, but looking closer, I realized that I was wrong.

"It's only got one side," I replied.

Mrs. Bradbury nodded, a proud smile lighting up her face.

"The Möbius strip doesn't have a front and back like a regular piece of paper, or an inside and outside like you'd find in an ordinary loop. The Möbius strip only has one side." Taking the twisted loop of paper from me, she started to trace an imaginary path with the tip of her finger. "If you could walk around this loop of paper, you'd think that it never comes to an end. The only difference you'd find is that the features on one side of your body would switch over to the other side as you moved around the closed curve."

Now, as my heart thuds beneath my fingertips, I realize what this means.

Maybe these stairs aren't never-ending but just twisted into a Möbius strip. I can't ever reach the top or the bottom because I'm stuck in an infinite loop.

I picture myself turning the Möbius strip over in my hand, the one-sided shape existing only in two dimensions. There's only one way to find the ends of the strip again—and that's to tear the paper in two.

Reaching down, I start to tug at the fraying carpet beneath my feet. At first it won't shift, but then I find a loose bit on the underside of the stair and, as I pull on it, the carpet comes away, exposing the bare floorboards underneath.

Scientists have spent hundreds of years searching for the smallest building blocks that are used to build reality. First they thought it was atoms; then they discovered that atoms were made out of protons, electrons, and neutrons; and then, when they started smashing these together, they found even smaller particles they gave weird names like quarks and gluons. Every time science thinks it's worked out what reality really is, it finds another layer of reality hiding underneath.

That's what I'm looking for now. What's hiding underneath.

Forcing my fingers into the gap between the floorboards, I try to pry them free. I feel the edge of the wood splinter against my fingernails, sharp jabs of pain forcing me to bite my lip. I pull with all my strength, but the floorboard doesn't move—the nails holding it in place are firmly hammered down.

With a howl of frustration, I pull my hand free. I can't take this anymore—all the strangeness, the impossibility of everything that I'm experiencing. I just want to find out what's really real. . . .

I start to pound the bare floorboards, feeling the wood splinter and crack with every strike of my fist. The pain that I feel tells me this is real, but as the stairs cascade into infinity, I know this can't be true. I catch the side of my little finger on the head of a nail near the floorboard's edge, gouging out a chunk of skin. And as the droplets of blood fly through the air like tiny red balloons, I watch reality splinter around me.

The floorboards beneath my feet dissolve into an inky blackness. The never-ending stairs with their long lines of Maisies disappear, leaving only an empty void behind. I screw my eyes shut, unable to comprehend this infinite blackness, and when I open them again, I find myself standing at the door to Lily's bedroom.

Then I hear her voice from inside.

"Come in."

"I've been doing some research," Lily says as we cross the bridge at the bottom of the street. Beneath the parapet, the railway tracks are empty, the hourly train that runs into town every Saturday slowly disappearing into the distance. The sky above is a perfect blue, the electric cables strung along the railway line almost glinting in the sunlight. "According to the internet, our health insurance won't cover tattoo removal, so this means I've got to find the money myself."

I hurry to keep up with my sister, Lily striding ahead almost as quickly as she's talking.

"I've looked on a couple of different websites, and it

costs as much as five hundred dollars to get a tattoo like mine removed. I've only got a hundred and fifty bucks in my bank account. And even if I'm able to save up enough money, apparently it can take months for the laser treatments to totally get rid of the tattoo."

She glances down at the Band-Aid that's stuck to the underside of her wrist.

"I wish I could just peel it off like a fake tattoo," she says bitterly.

As we reach the top of the bridge I can see the back of our house. The budget gazebo is now fully erected in the yard as it backs onto the railway line. And on the other side of the tracks the row of shops leads up Cheswick Hill, the bright sunshine making me squint as we start to descend the bridge.

"Maybe I can help," I say. "Grandma Pegg said she was going to send me some money for my birthday. You can have that when it comes. And if we both help Dad test his new video game, that'd be a way to get some extra cash."

Lily looks at me, her eyes shining in the bright sunlight.

"You'd do that for me?"

I nod.

"Of course I would," I tell her. "You're my sister."

As we walk, Lily reaches out to squeeze my hand.

"Thanks, Maisie."

Our shadows lead the way as we turn the corner at the bottom of the bridge. The railings that fence off the railway tracks are bent and broken in places, the metal posts forced apart by the teenage boys who hang out on the promenade at night, riding around on their bikes.

I watch them from my window sometimes when I'm supposed to have gone to sleep. With my bedroom light off, I can see them illuminated in the streetlights as they squeeze through the gap, playing chicken as they leave stuff lying on the railway tracks, waiting for the next passing train to squash these things flat.

If the railway line weren't here, we could get to the shops in just a couple of minutes by sneaking through the gap in our back fence.

"I don't know why Mom wouldn't let me go to the store on my own," I complain as we walk past the pharmacy that marks the start of the promenade. "I mean, I'm ten now."

Lily laughs.

"Mom wouldn't let me go to the store on my own until I'd started high school. And then as soon as she did, I was the one she kept sending on errands to buy milk and stuff whenever we ran out. You should count yourself lucky."

Outside the store, there're a couple of boys hanging around on their bikes, and as we pass, the taller one, who's wearing a cool T-shirt, wolf-whistles at Lily.

"All right, gorgeous," he says, wheeling his bike around to ride alongside us. "Give us a smile."

Lily just ignores him.

With his face tightening into a scowl, the boy pulls his bike around in a tight curve in front of us, forcing us to stop to avoid walking straight into him.

"I asked you to smile," the boy says, an angry tone now in his voice. "Didn't you hear?"

I glance up at my sister, feeling suddenly frightened, although I'm not exactly sure why.

For a second, Lily stands her ground, her eyes narrowing as she glares back at the boy. Then she pulls her face into a smile, so fake it hurts, but the boy must think this is real enough to count as he wheels off back to his friend.

Grabbing hold of my hand, Lily hurries me on as the boy on the bike mutters something I don't understand.

Lily blushes flame red.

"What did he mean?" I ask as the two boys behind us laugh.

"Don't worry," Lily says with a shake of her head. "You wouldn't understand."

There's so much I don't understand. Sometimes the way the universe works seems simple in comparison with people.

Reaching Kumar's Convenience Store, Lily pushes the door open, the ring of the bell above it announcing our arrival as we head inside.

"All right, girls?" Mrs. Kumar says, looking up from the box of drinks she's stacking in the glass-fronted fridge. Her bright red sari is pinned to her shoulder, and as she gets to her feet she brushes her hands down the front of it. "What can I get you today?"

"We need some paper plates," Lily replies, glancing up at the magazines on the racks. "Do you have any?"

Nodding, Mrs. Kumar points toward the back of the shop.

"Second shelf down on the right," she says. "Just past the trash bags."

I follow Lily as she heads down the aisle, ignoring the display of chocolate bars, even though I'm starting to feel a bit hungry again. I remember the mountains of food on the kitchen table. There'll be plenty to eat when my party gets started.

Picking up a pack of paper plates, Lily turns back to the front of the shop.

"Wait a second," I say, pointing to the soft drink bottles on the shelf below. "Didn't Mom want us to get some drinks too?"

Lily shakes her head.

"Mom's got a ton of drinks in the fridge. She was just saying that to stop you from moaning about me coming to the shop with you."

I can't believe it. Mom lied to me on my birthday.

"Don't stress," Lily says, noticing the frown on my face. She pulls the twenty-dollar bill out of her purse. "This means I can keep the change and put it toward the laser treatment I need to get the tattoo removed."

I should feel happy for Lily, but I can't help feeling kind of annoyed too as she turns toward the counter. I wish everyone would stop treating me like a little kid.

As Lily places the paper plates on the counter, Mrs. Kumar picks them up and scans them.

"Do you need a bag?" she asks.

"Yes, please."

Pulling one out from under the counter, Mrs. Kumar slides the paper plates into it.

"That'll be two dollars and fifty cents," she says, handing the bag to Lily. "Are you having a picnic with those paper plates? You've certainly got the weather for it today."

Lily shakes her head.

"It's Maisie's birthday. We're having a party."

The ever-present smile on Mrs. Kumar's face grows even wider.

"Happy birthday!" she says.

I just blush in reply. I wish Lily wouldn't embarrass me like this.

On a stand next to the counter, there's a display of Mylar balloons—red, blue, pink, purple, and gold—each one bobbing gently on its color-coded ribbon in the breeze from the air-conditioning unit overhead.

Mrs. Kumar reaches over the counter and pulls one of the balloons free. "A birthday balloon for the birthday girl." She beams as she presents it to me.

I can feel the blush on my face bloom to match the color of the balloon. If Mom and Dad getting me a birthday button wasn't bad enough, now Mrs. Kumar is giving me this little kid's toy. For a second, I think about saying no thanks, but then I realize that the helium inside the balloon might come in handy for one of my experiments. And at least it's not a pink one.

"Thanks, Mrs. Kumar," I say, looping the ribbon around my wrist. "And could I have a gold one too?" I add, an idea about how I could use two balloons starting to take shape in my brain.

Mrs. Kumar nods. "Of course you can. Help yourself, Maisie."

As I loop the second balloon around my wrist, Lily just grins.

"Come on, birthday girl."

With the red and gold balloons bobbing behind us, we walk back up the promenade. At first I'm a bit worried that we'll see those boys again, but I look outside the pharmacy and their bikes are gone. Breathing a sigh of relief, I glance up at Lily.

The sunlight bathes her skin in a golden sheen, and

as her long dark hair blows in the breeze, she almost looks like a grown-up.

"What do you want to be when you grow up?" I ask her.

Lily looks surprised.

"I dunno," she says, shaking her head. "Maybe work in fashion or something. What about you?"

There's so much I want to do. I'd like to work at the Large Hadron Collider and discover a new elementary particle. I want to solve the Riemann hypothesis—the most difficult problem in math—and win a million dollars. I might even set up my own tech company to research artificial intelligence. But Lily would think these dreams of mine just prove that I'm a freak.

"Maybe be a video game designer like Dad," I say finally. "Or win a gold medal in the hundred-meter at the Olympics."

Lily and I always used to have races in the backyard. She never let me win, but I bet I could beat her now that I'm ten.

Lily grins.

"Maybe you'd get a silver medal," she says. "But I'd definitely get gold." She wraps the handles of the plastic bag around her other wrist, holding it more tightly in her hand. "I'll race you home. First one inside the gazebo wins the Olympics. On your marks, get set, GO!"

Lily starts running, her sudden acceleration taking me

by surprise. With a squeal of protest, I start chasing after her, the helium balloons dancing behind me in the breeze. But Lily is racing ahead, her long legs easily outpacing my shorter ones as she reaches the bottom of the bridge.

"See you later, slowpoke," she calls over her shoulder.

I shake my head as Lily disappears around the corner. I've got to win this race.

I push open the bedroom door.

In front of me I see Lily's room, just exactly as it should be. The pale yellow walls slope down from the ceiling, her bookshelves and storage units tucked against the bottom. There's Lily's bed covered in a pastel-colored throw, the poster on the wall above it showing a picture of the Eiffel Tower.

A woman is sitting at Lily's desk beneath the sky-light window, her black bobbed hair hiding her face from view. For a second, I think it's Mom, but then the woman turns around, and I see with a sudden jolt of surprise that it's Lily.

There's a streak of gray at the front of her bangs like

a silver satin ribbon. As her gaze meets mine, Lily's eyes open wide, deepening the lines on her face. She looks even older than Mom.

At first I think this must be makeup for some kind of costume, even though Lily's just wearing a normal black top and jeans.

"Lily?" I ask, unable to process this picture of my sister. "Is that really you?"

"I'm sorry," Lily replies. "I didn't know if you'd recognize me like this." Her hand reaches up to her face in a self-conscious gesture. On her inner wrist I catch a glimpse of a black loop of ink, a tattoo of a Möbius strip. "I must look so old."

"I don't understand," I say, the sight in front of me even more confusing than everything I've seen so far. "What happened to you?"

A single tear creeps out of the corner of Lily's eye, and I watch it roll down her face.

"Life," she replies, brushing the tear away with the back of her hand. "Life happened to me."

I don't know what Lily means. She's only fifteen years old. She's got her whole life ahead of her—just like me.

This must be some kind of optical illusion, like that picture of an old lady where if you stare at it for long enough, you see a young woman appear instead. I just need to keep looking at Lily and she'll go back to how she's supposed to look.

"You've got to help me, Lily," I tell her, trying to force my brain to see things the right way. "You won't believe what's happening out there. There was an infinite staircase outside your bedroom and a black hole in the bathroom. Our house is being erased, and I don't know what I'm supposed to do."

I can't stop myself from crying, and through my tears I see Lily's face crumple too, the wrinkles on her forehead furrowing into a frown.

"It wasn't supposed to be like this," she says, shaking her head in disbelief. "I thought that deleting the code would just reset the reality. I didn't think it would have a physical manifestation in the virtual world and erase the house around you."

I don't know what Lily's talking about. This doesn't even sound like Lily.

"What do you mean, 'reset the reality'?"

Looking around the bedroom, Lily slowly wipes away her tears. Then she looks up at me.

"I'm sorry, Maisie, but none of this is real. This is a computer-generated reality."

I laugh out loud.

"That's ridiculous." I point to the birthday button that's pinned to my pajama top. "I know this is real," I tell her. "I've got my own reality check."

Taking the button off, I jab the pin into my finger, feeling the pain flare like a firework in my mind. Wincing,

I watch a droplet of blood well from the pinprick and thrust my hand forward for Lily to see.

"Look, I'm bleeding. This isn't *Fun Kart Fury*—this *is* reality."

Lily stares as the droplet of blood falls from my finger.

"That was one of Dad's games," she whispers. "It's been a long time since I thought about *Fun Kart Fury*."

The pain in my finger might be fading, but my confusion is only growing. Why's Lily talking like this? It might've been a few months since we last played *Fun Kart Fury*, but she's making it sound like it's been decades.

"And you're right," Lily continues, her voice barely more than a whisper still. "This isn't a video game. I wanted to make it better than that. I wanted to give you the ultimate virtual reality."

I look around the room. Everything seems so real—the study guides piled up next to Lily's bed, her makeup arranged in front of the dressing-table mirror, tiny specks of dust swirling in the beams of reflected sunlight. But then I look back at Lily's middle-aged face, and reality seems to fall apart again.

"But this is too complex for any computer to generate," I protest, scrabbling to make sense of what Lily's saying. I wave my hand through the air and watch the specks of dust dance. "Look," I say. "Even Dad couldn't model the random motion of these particles of dust. It would take hundreds of billions of teraflops of computer power. And that's not all: I can see, feel, hear, taste, and touch everything around me. My brain is processing trillions of bytes of information every second. There's no computer that's been built that could create a virtual reality like this."

"Maybe not when Dad was making video games," Lily replies with a mournful look in her eyes. "But computers have changed a lot since then. There's something called Moore's law, which predicts that computers become twice as powerful every two years. Everything that a computer allows you to do, from playing games to sending satellites into space, is controlled by its microchips. You know that computer chips used to consist of billions of tiny silicon switches that flicked on and off billions of times every second. All the information a computer uses is either a zero or a one—a binary code—depending on whether the switch is open or closed. But today's optical computers flow photons of light between the switches, meaning there's no limit to the amount of information they can process. An entire universe can be replicated in a single microchip."

My head's spinning as I try to make sense of this. Moore's law, binary code, computer chips powered by photons of light ... How does Lily even know any of this stuff? Her grades in science and computing are terrible—I'm the one who's supposed to be academically gifted.

I look at Lily's face, the lines around her hazel eyes creased in concern. I still don't know why she looks so old.

"If what you're telling me is true," I say, still trying to hold on to some sliver of reality, "then why have all these impossible things been happening? I've watched the kitchen expand to fill the universe. I've seen Mom's favorite glass cat get smashed to pieces and then put itself back together again. Outside the front door is an infinite blackness that makes my head hurt. If this is some kind of virtual reality, then why's it so weird? If you can fit the whole universe on a microchip, why isn't it finished?"

For a moment, Lily doesn't answer. She just sits there in silence, staring up at me through a brimming veil of tears.

"I got things mixed up," she says finally, her voice thick with emotion. "I activated your code before I finished building the world. And once I realized my mistake it was too late. You were awake."

"What do you mean?" I say, feeling even more confused than I was before. "I've been awake since my alarm clock went off at nine o'clock this morning. It's my birthday—I'm ten years old today. Don't you remember?"

Lily's really crying now, her shoulders heaving as she tries to hold herself together.

"I remember," she says, each word a stuttered sob. "I remember every moment of that day. Don't you, Maisie?"

Since I woke up this morning I've seen black holes and Möbius strip staircases, a tidal wave of nothingness wiping my home away, but as I stare at Lily's crumpled face, I'm starting to feel really scared.

I shake my head.

So Lily tells me, and I remember everything.

As Lily disappears around the corner of the bridge, I gradually slow to a breathless halt. I'm already starting to get a stitch. I really shouldn't have eaten that second banana pancake for breakfast.

I thought I'd be able to beat Lily now that I'm ten, but I was wrong. She'll be back home in five minutes flat, and I'll just feel like a little kid again.

Through the broken railings I can see the back of our house on the other side of the railway line. The back garden is hidden from view, but I can just catch a glimpse of white canvas through the gap in the fence that for weeks Dad's been promising Mom he'll get fixed. If I could take a shortcut across the tracks, I'd be inside the gazebo before Lily's even opened the front door.

When you grow up next to a railway line, you get a bit tired of your mom and dad telling you that you face certain death if you try to get your ball back when you've kicked it over the fence. To drum the message home, Mom once made me and Lily watch a health and safety film on YouTube that showed this boy getting hit by a train after he got the laces of his cleats caught on the track. Lily reckoned the film was from the 1970s because the boy had a really bad haircut, but she still stopped playing soccer in the garden with me after that.

I rest my hand against the fence, the metal railings bent back by the teenage boys who hang around on the promenade. I never see *them* get squashed flat when they sneak onto the tracks at night. Beneath the power lines that stretch overhead, the steel rails glint in the late-morning sunshine.

I glance at my watch. The next train's not due for another forty-five minutes. If I walk across quickly, I'll be at the back fence in just a couple of minutes. All I've got to do, then, is sneak through the gap there without Mom or Dad seeing, and Lily won't even know how I beat her home.

Ducking my head down, I squeeze through the railings. Sacks of gravel are piled up immediately in front of me, but skirting around the edge of them, I can see a straight path to the other side of the tracks. There's a traffic cone abandoned halfway across, left over from the last time the bicycle fools tried to play chicken with a train.

Lily says I don't know what real life is like, but as the loose stones crunch under my sneakers I know that she's wrong. I can feel the sun beating down, sweat causing the ribbons around my wrist to stick to my skin. The sun is a star ninety-three million miles away, and everyone on this planet is falling around it at over sixty thousand miles per hour. With every step that I take, we're zooming through the vacuum of space into an ever-expanding universe. Life is an adventure, and as I cross the tracks I feel so *alive*.

Stepping over the steel rails, I look up into the clear blue sky, and that's when I see the gold balloon touch the power line.

BANG!

The sound of it starts at the *B* and then stretches into infinity. A bang so loud it instantly makes me forget everything else. The noise seems to come from every direction at once, inside and out. A bright white light surrounds me like a galaxy of stars being born. And then I feel the pain.

My muscles clench, my body locking up in agony as a burning fire sears through my veins. Inside my head I'm screaming as every pain receptor sends a simultaneous signal to my brain. I can smell burning from somewhere, and then I realize it's me.

In what seems like slow motion, I crumple to the ground, my gaze still fixed to the sky.

In the human body, there are three essential components that keep you alive. Your heart, which pumps blood around your body; the blood vessels—arteries, veins, and capillaries—which carry this blood to every cell inside you; and the blood itself, delivering the oxygen and nutrients you need to keep you alive. This is your circulatory system, and it stretches for about sixty thousand miles inside you. And every inch of mine is burning with a living fire. The pain is excruciating.

Through white-hot eyes, I watch the red balloon float up into the sky. The ribbon holding it to my wrist must have burned through. But that doesn't matter now.

My body is stopped, trapped inside this bubble of pain. It feels like now is forever.

Between zero and one there is an infinity of numbers: 0.1, 0.01, 0.101 . . . The numbers go on forever, stretching past the decimal point into infinity.

The helium balloon is getting smaller, dwindling to a red teardrop as it rises high in the sky.

My eyelids flicker, the only part of my body that I seem to be able to move. The pain is slowly starting to fade, but it's leaving behind a terrible cold.

I blink and start counting to infinity.

And then I see darkness.

15

"So I'm dead?"

Still sitting at her desk, Lily looks up at me with eyes that have seen too much. She nods, tears still sliding down her face.

"When you didn't come home, we all went out looking for you—Mom, Dad, me. We were walking back over the bridge toward the store, calling out your name. I was the one who saw you lying next to the railway line."

Lily's face crumples in pain as she relives the memory again.

"Your helium balloon must have hit one of the power lines. The ambulance came, but there was nothing they could do. The paramedics said you would've died instantly."

I remember the white light surrounding me. Twenty-five thousand volts of electricity sent surging through my body. An instant that lasted for infinity.

Lily shakes her head, a loose strand of gray hair falling across her tearstained face.

"Why were you even on the tracks, Maisie?"

I'm crying now too. How could I have been so stupid? The answer tears me apart even as I speak it out loud.

"I just wanted to beat you home."

Lily's shoulders shake as a fresh wave of sobs racks her frame.

I remember Lily sitting on the edge of the bath on the morning of my birthday, her whole body shaking as she stared at the tattoo on her wrist. She might look like a grown-up now, but I can still see my teenage sister sobbing inside. But this time I don't know what to say to stop her from crying. I don't even know how to stop myself from crying.

"Lily . . ."

"Mom and Dad blamed me for the accident," she sobs. "They said I should've never left you on your own."

It wasn't Lily's fault, but all I can think about now is Mom and Dad.

"Where are they?" I ask, barely able to get the words out.

"Dad passed away last year," Lily replies, her voice still shaking. "He was only sixty-two, but the cancer came back. That's when I moved in with Mom. She hasn't been coping that well. I think she's starting to forget stuff, just like Grandma Pegg used to. . . ."

Lily's words trail off as she buries her head in her hands.

I feel numb.

Inside a computer chip, information can be stored as either a zero or a one—on or off—yes or no. But inside my head, every single switch is screaming out a single word. *NO!*

I can't speak, unable to process everything that Lily has told me.

Lifting her head to see my broken expression, Lily reaches out a hand toward me. On the underside of her wrist I see the tattoo of the Möbius strip, its edges blurred where the ink has faded over time.

"I'm sorry, Maisie," she says, rising to her feet. "It wasn't meant to be like this."

Through the skylight window I can see the sun shining down out of a clear blue sky, but there's no warmth to it. It's just like a picture plastered over the cracks that let the dark in.

"What *is* this?" I sob.

"My life's work," Lily replies, the lines on her face

softening around the corners of her mouth. "A simulated universe where we could be together again."

Lily gestures toward the laptop computer that's behind her on the desk.

"Everything you can see, everything that you hear, everything you taste, smell, and touch is part of this computer-generated reality. After you died, Maisie, I felt I owed it to you to follow your dream. I studied computing in college, learned as much as I could from Dad about video game design and how to build a virtual world. And as computers got more powerful, the complexity of the world I could create grew too. Our house, our street, our town, our lives—all starting again on the day you left us behind."

I stare at my big sister, now looking even older than Mom. It's like Lily has been trying to live my life for me.

"But you wanted to work in fashion," I say.

"It's not really that different," Lily replies with a wry smile. "It's all about design. And besides, I've managed to drop in a few fashion tips here and there."

She points toward the top pocket of my pajamas, and glancing down, I notice for the first time the designer label that's stitched there.

Reaching up, I run my finger over the stitching, feeling the letters spell out a very fashionable name. A tiny smear of red underlines it as a fresh droplet of blood weeps from the pinprick on my finger. I wince, worrying that it won't come out in the wash, but then I realize that I don't have anything to worry about now.

It's not real.

I look down at the tip of my finger, every line and whorl of my fingerprint completely unique. If this is a computer-generated reality, what does that make me?

"Am I real?" I ask.

Lily nods.

"You are to me."

Inside my head, I flick through my memories. Snuggling up with Mom as we read stories on the sofa, kicking a ball in the back garden with Dad, starting school, quitting school, sitting at the table with Mrs. Bradbury as she taught me about the universe. I remember playing *Fun Kart Fury* with Lily, the two of us collapsing in laughter as our video game characters farted their way around the track. How can I remember any of this if none of this is real?

I don't even have to ask the question out loud before Lily starts to answer.

"When the ambulance came, Mom and Dad begged them to save you. The paramedics couldn't find a heartbeat, but they still hooked you up to their life-support machines to do everything they could. You'd stopped breathing, there was no pulse, no sign that you were still alive, but the EEG recording still showed brain waves, even after you were clinically dead. A delta wave burst of brain activity that slowly faded into nothingness. Dad managed to download this before it disappeared."

Lily's gaze searches mine, wanting to make sure I understand.

"Since you've been gone, Maisie, scientists have learned so much about how the brain works. They've mapped the eighty-six billion neurons that make up the human mind, discovering exactly how these cells communicate information by sending electrical charges to each other—just like the transistors inside a computer chip—and decoding the thoughts these sparks create. With the help of a friend of mine who's a neuroscientist, I managed to take the recording of your brain activity that Dad downloaded and turn it into data, the beginning of the code that makes you *you*."

In my head, I remember the red balloon rising up into the clear blue sky.

"Then all I had to do was fill in the gaps," Lily continues. "My memories of you, Mom's and Dad's too, your diaries, your experiments, even your university work. Pictures and photos, family videos—all turned into data and added to the code."

I should be angry at the thought of Lily reading my diaries, but this doesn't seem to matter now.

"I just wanted to put things right, Maisie," Lily says, her face stained with tears. "I just wanted the chance to play with you again."

I feel stunned, the realization slowly dawning. I'm standing in the middle of Lily's bedroom, but if what Lily's telling me is true, then this is all contained on a computer chip—even me. Pythagoras thought the whole universe was built out of numbers, and now I realize he was right. My universe is made of zeroes and ones.

"I'm so sorry, Maisie," Lily continues, her voice still raw with tears. "Mom and Dad were right. I should never have run off without you."

The silver streak in her bangs frames Lily's face as it crumples again.

"It wasn't your fault," I tell her, my heart breaking as I see the pain my sister has been carrying for so long come pouring out. "I was supposed to be the clever one, but I did something so stupid."

I reach out to hug Lily, but my arms fall right through her. It's like trying to hug sunlight.

"This is just my avatar," Lily sobs apologetically as I stagger back in surprise. "After everything went wrong, I didn't have the time to add myself properly to the virtual world. Not how I used to be, anyway. I just wanted to give you this second chance of life, but I've made such a mess of things."

I shake my head, my own tears rolling down my face.

"You haven't made a mess of things," I tell her, still astounded by Lily's achievement. "This is the best game I've ever played."

When Lily and I used to play *Fun Kart Fury*, there was another bug that we found, but instead of just making a silly farting sound when you tried to accelerate, this glitch gave you infinite lives. That's what Lily has given me now. She's given me infinite lives.

But it's not enough.

I look at my sister, her face lined with worry. I need her to know that I'm so grateful for what she's done. Reaching out with my hand, I gently stroke her face, my fingers shimmering as they trace the line of her reflection. I can almost feel the warmth of her skin as the zeroes and ones fire in my brain.

"Thank you, Lily. For everything."

And then I turn around and open the bedroom door.

"Maisie!"

My sister's shout snaps into silence as I stare into the void.

An infinite darkness stares back at me.

Black holes are created when a giant star dies. After using up all the fuel that powers the process of nuclear fusion, the center of the star collapses in upon itself, causing a massive explosion that blasts part of the star into space.

All the matter that's left then gets squeezed into a tiny point to create a black hole.

That's what I'm looking at now. My life exploded when the balloon hit the power line, leaving behind this infinite blackness.

The gravity inside a black hole is so strong that nothing can escape. No light, no matter, not even information. And at the heart of a black hole is a point of infinite density—a tiny speck even smaller than an atom—where even the laws that describe how the universe works break down. This is called the singularity.

I shiver as I stand on the edge of the event horizon, a thin sliver of space-time separating me from the irresistible pull of the black hole. Just one step forward and I'm never coming back. I glance over my shoulder to see Lily, her hand still reaching out toward me, this action frozen in a single moment of time.

Then I turn back toward the black hole waiting for me outside the door.

Some scientists think the singularity at the heart of a black hole might hold the answers to the mysteries of the universe. Maybe it's time somebody found out if this is true.

Closing my eyes, I step forward into the singularity and surrender to forever.

16

Through the broken railings I can see the back of my house on the other side of the railway line, the white canvas of the budget gazebo flapping through a gap in the fence.

I'm back on the other side of the railway bridge as Lily runs home, and I know what happens next.

I can feel the warmth of the metal railing under my fingers as I rest my hand against the fence, but as I scream at myself to turn around, my mind doesn't seem to be listening. It's like I'm trapped inside my own head, powerless to act as I glance down at my watch and then squeeze through the railings.

Sacks of gravel are piled up immediately in front of

133

me, but my feet seem to know the path they want to follow, skirting the sacks as I silently scream at them to stop.

I don't know what's happening to me. When I stepped into the singularity, I thought I'd find oblivion. I should've been crushed by the weight of gravity, my body stretched and spaghettified as I was sucked into the black hole. Instead it's brought me back here to the moment of my death.

My mind recoils in fear. Is the infinity at the heart of the black hole going to make me relive this again and again and again?

Loose stones crunch under my sneakers as I walk across the tracks. I'm nearly a third of the way there now, my eyes fixed straight ahead as I send desperate signals to my brain to stop. It's like I'm a passenger in my own body, strapped into the child seat in the back, unable to grab hold of the wheel as the driver accelerates toward the crash barrier at full speed.

Ahead of me, the steel rails gleam under the summer sunshine. Around my wrist the ribbons of the balloons are slick with sweat, and I know what comes next. . . .

I tense myself, waiting for the inevitable explosion when the balloon touches the power line overhead.

Then I hear a shout from directly behind me, my sister's voice raised in an anguished scream.

"Maisie!"

Turning around, I see Lily, her face ash white as she grabs hold of my hand. With a single action, she rips the ribbons from my wrist, letting them go as the balloons float up into the sky.

Looking up, I see an arc of electricity shoot out from the power line, zapping the gold balloon. A blinding flash so bright that it hurts my eyes.

BANG!

The sound of this explosion seems to jolt my mind back into my body. Raising my hand to shield my eyes, I watch as a gentle rain of shredded aluminum foil falls from the sky. Some of these scraps are still burning, shining like embers as, above the power lines, the surviving red balloon soars up into the open sky.

"What are you doing?" Lily shouts, shaking me hard. "That could've been you!"

I stare dumbfounded at my sister, her face unlined with age.

She's fifteen again, and I'm still alive.

Lily looks at me, her anger incandescent.

Then we both burst into tears.

Lily wraps her arms around me, hugging me tight. I hug her back, burying my face in her hair. Sweat sticks it to my cheek, but I just don't care.

"I'm sorry, Maisie," Lily sobs. "I should never have run off without you."

"Don't be silly," I tell her, unable to believe that I can hold my sister again. "I'm the stupid one. I don't know what I was thinking trying to get across the tracks. I just wanted to beat you back home."

These final words dissolve into sobs as Lily gently shushes my tears.

We hold each other tightly, clinging on as the world spins at nearly a thousand miles per hour.

"Don't tell Mom and Dad what just happened," Lily says finally, her voice hot in my ear. "They'd kill me if they knew I'd left you on your own."

I shake my head, unable to stop a nervous giggle from escaping from my lips.

"I think they'd kill me too."

Lily snorts in reply, and before I know it, we're both laughing, a wave of hysteria overtaking us that slowly wipes our tears away. Finally letting go of the hug, we stand there for a moment, another secret shared bringing us closer together.

The sun is shining down overhead, our shadows truncated as they stretch across the loose stones. Then Lily casts a nervous glance up the tracks.

"Come on," she says, looping her arm around my shoulder. "Let's go home."

We start to walk back toward the fence, sunlight bathing the broken railings in a golden light.

Scientists don't know what's inside the heart of a black hole. When I stepped into the singularity, the laws of physics as we know them broke down. The Big Bang theory says that our universe began as an infinitely small point containing an infinitely huge amount of matter. Just like the singularity at the heart of a black hole.

Maybe that's all our universe is—a tiny speck inside another black hole. From the outside our universe might look infinitely small, but from the inside it would look infinite. Maybe that's where I am now.

As we squeeze through the railings and start to walk back over the bridge, I think about what this means. Lily is right by my side, the shopping bag with the party plates swinging between us. As we near the top of the bridge, I can see the back of our house. The gazebo is standing proudly in the back garden, ready for my birthday party, and through the patio doors I can see Mom and Dad in the kitchen.

The reality is our universe is made of elementary particles. Everything that exists is built from these smallest building blocks. Mom, Dad, Lily, and I are just electrons and quarks stuck together with the help of gluons and photons. But when you get down to these tiny particles and look even closer, all you'll find is numbers.

This is why scientists have to be supergood at math. The universe is built out of numbers.

I don't know if I'm still inside the computer-generated reality that Lily built for me. But some scientists think our universe might just be a hologram. According to Mrs. Bradbury, these scientists think zeroes and ones are the only things that are really real. . . .

Lily squeezes my hand as we cross the bridge. I look up at my sister and smile. I can hear the birds singing in the trees and feel the sunshine on my skin as we walk together hand in hand.

I don't know what's really real, but then, nobody does. All I know is I'm ten years old and I'm walking home with my big sister to get ready for my birthday party.

It's going to be the best day ever.

```
01001000 01100101 00100000 01110111 01101000
01101111 00100000 01100010 01101001 01101110
01100100 01110011 00100000 01110100 01101111
00100000 01101000 01101001 01101101 01110011
01100101 01101100 01100110 00100000 01100001
00100000 01101010 01101111 01111001 00100000
00001101 00001010 01000100 01101111 01100101
01110011 00100000 01110100 01101000 01100101
00100000 01110111 01101001 01101110 01100111
01100101 01100100 00100000 01101100 01101001
01100110 01100101 00100000 01100100 01100101
01110011 01110100 01110010 01101111 01111001
00001101 00001010 01000010 01110101 01110100
00100000 01101000 01100101 00100000 01110111
01101000 01101111 00100000 01101011 01101001
01110011 01110011 01100101 01110011 00100000
01110100 01101000 01100101 00100000 01101010
01101111 01111001 00100000 01100001 01110011
00100000 01101001 01110100 00100000 01100110
01101100 01101001 01100101 01110011 00001101
00001010 01001100 01101001 01110110 01100101
01110011 00100000 01101001 01101110 00100000
01100101 01110100 01100101 01110010 01101110
01101001 01110100 01111001 11100010 10000000
10011001 01110011 00100000 01110011 01110101
01101110 01110010 01101001 01110011 01100101
```

139

The Science of
The Infinite Lives of Maisie Day

There's a lot of fascinating science in *The Infinite Lives of Maisie Day*, from the Big Bang that started the universe to what exactly you'd find inside a black hole. Some of these ideas can stretch the brains of real-life scientists, so let's take a look to find out more!

We'll start with something simple: What exactly is the universe?

The universe is everything that exists—all the stars and galaxies in the sky—and when you look at it now, it's pretty big. But most scientists think that our universe started out as a tiny seed—a minuscule speck of space-time a trillion trillion trillion times smaller than a grain of sand. This tiny seed contained all the energy and matter that would eventually create everything in the universe.

And 13.8 billion years ago, this tiny speck of space-time suddenly got very big, very fast in a cosmic event scientists call the Big Bang.

So could you say this was some kind of intergalactic rock concert?

Not quite. The Big Bang was a super-hot explosion that started the universe. In less than a second, the universe grew from a tiny speck the size of a subatomic particle to a space thousands of miles across. And since then it has just kept on growing. We can only see the bit of the universe whose light has had the chance to reach us since the Big Bang. This is called the observable universe. It measures 93 billion light-years across and contains trillions of galaxies, but the whole universe is much, much bigger than that. Scientists are still working on understanding the ongoing expansion of the universe.

Does the universe go on forever?

We don't know. Some scientists think we might live in an infinite universe that stretches on forever in every direction, but others believe the universe must be finite and just have a particular shape that makes it look like it's infinite. According to these scientists, the universe might be shaped like a four-dimensional sphere or a saddle or even a doughnut!

Mmmm, round like a doughnut ...

This doesn't mean that our universe could be devoured at any second by an infinite number of four-dimensional Homer Simpsons. A weird doughnut-shaped universe would appear to be infinite because you could never reach the edge of it. If you traveled far enough in any direction, you'd just end up back at the point where you started.

Like a Möbius strip?

That's right. And you can even make a Möbius strip yourself to check this out—all you need is a strip of paper. A normal piece of paper has two sides: the front and the back. But if you give a strip of paper a twist and then join the ends together, you've created a Möbius strip. If you get a pen and draw a line down the center of your Möbius strip, you'll end up going twice around the loop before you reach the point you started from. And that's not the strangest thing. If you were able to walk around this loop of paper holding an egg in your right hand, by the time you got halfway around the Möbius strip you'd find that you were holding the egg in your left hand instead. Walking around the Möbius strip would turn you into a mirror image of yourself.

Wow! That's amazing!

There's more. . . . The egg you're holding is made out of atoms. That's not a surprise. Everything in the universe is made out of atoms. But at the moment, all the atoms in your egg are arranged in a particular way. This makes it, well, egg-shaped.

Oops! Er, I'm afraid I dropped the egg. . . .

Don't worry, I *knew* you were going to do that. But the smashed egg is still made of exactly the same atoms as before, only now they're disorganized and random. This means the *entropy* of the egg has increased.

Entropy is how random and disorganized something is.

Right. When the egg was whole, its atoms were arranged in a highly organized way, but when you dropped the egg, there were many different ways in which it could break. The atoms in this bit of shell could have ended up over here or over here or over here. There were so many different ways its atoms could be arranged—but it would still be a broken egg. Or think about an ice cube, where all the molecules are arranged to create a perfect cube shape. If you melt the ice cube, the molecules are able to move around more freely as a liquid. This means its entropy has increased. In the universe, entropy is always increasing. This is the second law of thermodynamics.

Thermodynamics?

Thermodynamics is a big word that means the bit of science that's all about heat and other forms of energy. The second law of thermodynamics says the level of disorder in the universe is steadily increasing. Eggs break, ice melts, stars burn themselves out and sometimes even become black holes.

Black holes! How could I make a black hole?

Black holes are created when a giant star dies. After using up all the fuel that powers the process of nuclear fusion, the heart of the star collapses in upon itself, causing a massive explosion that blasts part of the star into space. All the matter that's left then gets squeezed into a tiny point to create a black hole. The gravity inside a black hole is so strong that nothing can escape. Not even light.

And if you get too close and cross the *event horizon*—the boundary in space beyond which there's no escape from the black hole's gravity—then you'll find yourself falling into a bottomless pit.

You're kind of scaring me. So what exactly would happen if I fell into a black hole?

The immense gravity of the black hole warps space-time so much that the closer you get to a black hole, the slower time goes. You wouldn't necessarily notice time slowing down as you fell in, as the gravitational forces would stretch and squeeze you into a long, thin shape, essentially turning you into spaghetti!

What if I managed to escape being turned into spaghetti? What would I find inside the black hole?

Let's say you somehow survive this "spaghettification" and reach the heart of the black hole. There you'll find a point of infinite density—a tiny speck even smaller than an atom—where time and space come to an end. This is called the *singularity*.

Wait a second—a tiny speck even smaller than an atom? Isn't that where we started before the Big Bang?

That's right. And that makes some scientists think our universe might even have been born inside a black hole in another universe. Like Maisie says, from the outside our universe might look infinitely small, but to us on the inside it would look infinite.

Science explores the big questions about life, the universe, and everything—the same questions that can underpin the very best stories. Why are we here? What makes us human? How do we know we really exist? My other two novels, *The Many Worlds of Albie Bright* and *The Jamie Drake Equation*, are also inspired by scientific theories. I hope these stories help you to understand more about the world we all live in and inspire you to build a better one.

Acknowledgments

Science and stories both help us make sense of the world, and I'd like to thank the authors of the following books for expanding my understanding of reality: *A Brief History of Time* by Stephen Hawking, *Reality Is Not What It Seems* by Carlo Rovelli, *Our Mathematical Universe* by Max Tegmark, *Human Universe* by Brian Cox and Andrew Cohen, *Universal: A Guide to the Cosmos* by Brian Cox and Jeff Forshaw, *Cosmos* by Carl Sagan, *The Universe in Your Hand* by Christophe Galfard, *The Unknown Universe* by Stuart Clark, *The Infinite Book* by John D. Barrow, and *A Brief History of Infinity* by Brian Clegg. I'm also indebted to the authors of countless articles in *New Scientist* and *BBC Focus* magazines, as well as the makers of programs such as *Horizon* and *The Infinite Monkey Cage*, who help bring science to life for me. Thank you too to Alom Shaha, Helen Czerski, Ian Hamerton, and Olly Smith for their scientific guidance and advice. Any scientific errors or exaggerations remaining in the text are, of course, my own, and reflect Maisie's understanding of the scientific theories and ideas explored.

It took more than one person to turn a story that lives on the hard drive of my mind into the book that you're holding in your hands. I'd like to thank my wonderful editor, Kirsty Stansfield, for her sage words of advice and my fantastic agent, Lucy Juckes, for all her support. Thank you too to Fi, Catherine, Clare, Nicola, Hester, Rebecca, Kate, Ola, Tom, Jess, and all the team at Nosy Crow, as well as Beverly Horowitz and Rebecca Gudelis at my wonderful U.S. publisher, Delacorte Press.

Finally, I'd like to thank my family for all their love, support, and understanding. I couldn't have written this story without you.

About the Author

CHRISTOPHER EDGE grew up in Manchester, England, where he spent most of his childhood in the local library, dreaming up stories. He now lives in Gloucestershire, where he spends most of his time in the local library, dreaming up stories. His award-winning novel *The Many Worlds of Albie Bright* was named a Best Children's Book by the New York Public Library and was nominated for the prestigious CILIP Carnegie Medal in the UK, as was *The Jamie Drake Equation*.

christopheredge.co.uk

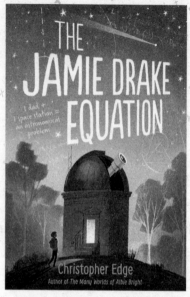

For anyone who has ever looked at
the stars and wondered.

★"With solid science and believable family conflicts, this will
be very satisfying to readers whose wishful thinking can suspend
disbelief." —*Kirkus Reviews*, Starred

"For beginner sci-fi readers or any child interested in aliens and
space flight." —*School Library Journal*

"Nimbly intertwines science, math, and fiction. Fiction enter-
tainingly edges out science . . . in a fantastical finale."
—*Publishers Weekly*

"Jamie's first-person narrative will draw readers into the story
and surprise them with twists along the way as its space-age
realism bends toward science fiction." —*Booklist*

"Thrilling, smart and surprisingly poignant . . . will leave young
readers with a hunger to know more about the universe and our
planet's place in it." —*BookPage*